S

THE SPY WHO BARKED
IN THE NIGHT

THE SPY WHO BARKED IN THE NIGHT

MARC LOVELL

PUBLISHED FOR THE CRIME CLUB BY
DOUBLEDAY & COMPANY, INC.
GARDEN CITY, NEW YORK
1986

All of the characters in this book
are fictitious, and any resemblance
to actual persons, living or dead,
is purely coincidental.

Library of Congress Cataloging-in-Publication Data

Lovell, Marc.
The spy who barked in the night.

I. Title.
PR6062.O853S697   1986   823'.914   85-13176
ISBN 0-385-23261-6

THE SPY WHO BARKED
IN THE NIGHT

ONE

Ethel sped around a corner. She squealed as she went. On the straight she increased her pace and in doing so trembled, but only slightly. Ethel was on wheels.

They were painted red. Too strong a red for the stripe of orange that ran around the body, which was pale green, just as the whole colour ensemble was too frivolous for the style: high and square and formal. Ethel was a London taxi, now retired.

Apple changed gear on approaching another corner. The speedometer needle touched a risky thirty-five miles per hour, yet Apple raced on, urgently and fumingly. He was late.

People on the East End street turned to stare as Ethel took the bend noisily. Apple, too fraught to enjoy the envy, expected they would be thinking that he had purposely kept his tyres low on air to create that dramatic squealing. He had known at the time that it wasn't a good idea.

Driving on, Apple seethed at the traffic. In fact, it was not all that dense. Nor was Apple all that late (one minute and forty seconds on last check). But, as he knew, you had to get the most you could out of every mission.

Possible mission, Apple amended.

"Can we talk?" Angus Watkin had asked last night when he telephoned to the Bloomsbury flat.

Apple fumbled: "Yes, sir. Of course. I mean yes, I'm clean." He hadn't heard from his Control in months.

With no further preamble Watkin said, "I may have a little errand for you." That was spookspeak for "an espionage oper-

ation." "I assume that you will be available in the morning
and for some time thereafter?"

Apple ignored the faint flavour of garlic in the dull soup of
his Control's voice. He was so stimulated that he even felt a
twinge of affection for Angus Watkin. Brutalising that away as
absurd, he said, "Being a senior official at the United Kingdom
Philological Institute, sir, I'm allowed a great deal of freedom
in the matter of time off." Which his chief knew, since he had
arranged that permanent cover himself. But Watkin was like
that.

Apple added, "And I was going to take tomorrow morning
off anyway, as it happens." That lie, he felt, though it wouldn't
be believed, chimed just the right note of servitude without full
subjection. His conscience had need of it.

"Therefore we can count on your presence at 10 A.M. sharp,
Porter," Angus Watkin said. He gave a number, a street name,
a district in the East End. After a repeat he asked, "Absorbed?"

Apple would never forget it. "Yes, sir."

"At that place you will do still more absorbing. You will do
it thoroughly. You will absorb until you begin to feel queasy."

"Yes, sir, and then leave."

"No, Porter. That is when the real absorption begins. You
will stay until it starts to make you suffer emotional stress."

"Yes, sir, of course."

Angus Watkin said, "The subject is a man. Of whom more
later, should that be the way matters go."

"You mean, sir, if this develops into a full mission."

"I dare say I do, Porter," Watkin said. With typical abrupt-
ness he tacked on a clipped, "Good night."

For Apple the night had been bad. Sleep had proved elusive
as he dwelled at length on being out in the field on a caper,
with his imaginings getting steadily more exotic and improbable. Between reveries he had suffered bouts of despondency,

thinking that the deal would either not come off at all or would turn out to be a lowly affair. Some jobs consisted merely of nodding at someone who was leaning on a lamppost.

This morning Apple would have had plenty of time if he hadn't wasted so much of it in pretending that he had all the time in the world. He had lazed around as though he knew there was no caper in the offing, which, he had hoped, would prevent him from being disappointed later.

Only when there had been a quarter of an hour to go had Apple flung pretence aside and started to bustle like somebody who had sat in a beehive.

He was bustling still. His face twitched and his limbs were constantly on the move as he tried to make up the lost time. Effort caused his precious vehicle to alternate groans with trembles, thus adding guilt to Apple's agitation.

Pedestrians did double and triple takes at Ethel, while others stopped in the summer sunlight to watch her go by. It wasn't every day you got to see a bit of circus equipment that had strayed from the pack, even though its driver formed a definite let-down.

Apple was plain fare, a dull-edged contrast to the colour around him, which he would have gladly donned had he owned sufficient courage.

What Apple owned in greatest measure was height. This he dressed in cowed shades of grey and styles that were fiercely last-year-but-one Establishment. His ties had even less gaiety. Add a manner which was on the verge of being apologetic, and the frame had little to recommend it, except to people who were almost as tall, to whom it was a solace.

Above was better, though hardly an aspect of flamboyance. Apple had a pale complexion. It showed clearly his sprinkling of freckles, whose gingery hue matched the neat-cut hair. The strongest colour present was that of his eyes, a green like spring grass. This prevented a wash-out of the whole face, which had neat, standard, amiable features, like medium-priced furniture.

Apple cut around a bus with a muttered "Excuse me." In answer to the oath hurled at him by the bus driver, he smiled his worldliness, tightly. Ethel raced on.

The next moment Apple had to do a rapid slow: he had seen the name-plate he wanted. With more consideration, calmer now, he steered Ethel around the last corner.

It was a seedy street, as drab as a vegetable garden in the rain. Its buildings, a hundred years old, had mostly stopped being homes and had crept stealthily into offices. They gave themselves away with small brass plates.

Apple found a place to park. He locked Ethel carefully before walking on, in the direction indicated by door numbers. As with all proud car owners he glanced back from a distance.

The right doorway led Apple into a vestibule. Its inner door said jadedly MINISTRY OF THE ENVIRONMENT. DEPARTMENT TWO. PLEASE KNOCK. Every o in the lettering had a face drawn on it.

Apple knocked, after counting the os, as any reader would. While waiting he put his watch back to the right time.

The door was opened by a man as drab and unwelcoming as the street. His articulate head movements took Apple past him and inside and along a passage; his bloated voice mentioned a door at the foot of the stairs.

Apple descended to that point. He pushed open the door, above which glowed a red light, and went to the movies.

The screen was flashing brightly, sound crashed on all sides. Faintly unnerved, feeling that he had stepped into a no man's land, Apple stood at the carpeted threshold to get his bearings.

The place was a projection-room. Dark as a black dog between flashes, it equalled in size a large living-room and had squat armchairs on either side of a centre aisle.

On the screen, boom and brightness were fading. They had been part of a New York street scene. Now on came a silent shot that had obviously been taken with a telescope-lens. It was of a man walking in a park. Details were blurred.

Settled, Apple was about to move from the head of the aisle, take a seat, when he noticed that he didn't have the projection-room entirely to himself.

There were two men. They sat midway along, opposite each other in aisle chairs.

Again Apple stopped when on the point of moving. This time it was because one of the men spoke. Turning to face the other, he said, "Porter's late."

While semi-watching the screen, where the facade of a typical Amsterdam house had replaced the park, Apple wondered what he ought to say to announce his presence.

After mumbling, the other agent also turned to his colleague. Apple didn't try for an identification from the pair of profiles. He had met too few people in the Service for it to be likely that he knew the pair.

A man was coming out onto the Amsterdam street as the second agent spoke. He asked, "What's he like, this Appleton Porter?"

Apple, being exceeding human, would not now have announced his presence for the world. He didn't move a muscle as he waited to hear the response.

It was a return question: "Which d'you want first, the good news or the bad news?"

"I'll take the good."

Both operatives faced the screen as it flicked to a close shot of the man running off along the street. When Amsterdam was replaced by a film of people at a dining-table, the agents turned away. They continued to switch back and forth throughout their exchange, which was dawdly, full of pauses.

The first agent said, "Porter's a speakfreak. Has about a

dozen languages spit-perfect, plus a dozen more in which he's merely fantastic."

"Lucky bastard."

Had Apple been in this conversation, he would have pointed out that it was more a matter of application than luck, though he would probably have made no comment on what flattered —the exaggeration. His perfect languages numbered seven.

Apple kept silent and still. Part of his attention he continued to hold on the screen (where the camera was favouring one of the male diners), mainly because this helped him to ignore the fact that he was eavesdropping.

"So go on," the second agent said. "Give me the rest of the good news."

"That's it, Stan. The guy's a star at foreign gab."

"How about the bad? Is it truly putrid?"

"Well look, he's a faceless one," the first agent said. "He is not, in a word, a pro."

"Oh dear."

Apple smiled loosely, sadly. He told himself he had to interrupt the operatives, at once, before it got worse, as truth had a habit of doing.

Also, Apple thought, it would be mortifying for the pair, as well as for himself, if they should see him, which could be any moment now, if they happened to turn their heads a fraction more. It was mortifying enough for his position in the moral niceties that he should be listening to a private conversation.

Apple realised that he was letting his semi-attention stray from the screen, where the camera eye, he now noted, was being blocked from a full view of the favoured man's face by another diner's head. Apple allowed his visual attention to go on straying.

The first agent said, "And there's the little matter of Porter's height, if I may use that adjective." He added after a significant pause, "He's six feet seven inches tall."

The second operative swayed sideways with, "You, Rex, are putting me on."

"I swear on my mother's life."

"Christ. And old Angus actually uses him?"

"Rarely, apart from the language connection, which amounts to doing delicate translations and high-level interpreting jobs. But yes, he does use him."

The second agent asked, "How can such a giraffe possibly go unnoticed, mingle with the mass?"

"Search me," the other man said. "But that's not all in the minus department."

"Go on, frighten me. It's been a slow morning."

"How about if I tell you that Appleton Porter has a habit of blushing? Also of collecting bits and pieces of useless data?"

Both men looked at the screen as, accompanied by a blare of jangly music, it switched from black/white dining-room to the colour and hustle of a fairground. Among the people strolling there was a man who was eating candy-floss.

Which man, Apple noted with care to stall the familiar heat which had prickled into existence on his chest, was the same person as in the other shots.

Turning away from the screen again, the pair of agents agreed that the repetition of film-clips was getting to be decidedly sickening. One suggested calling it a day. The other said, "Let's give it once more around the schoolyard, Stan, while I tell you the rest of the Appleton Porter story."

"I think I've had enough of that as well, thanks. And we might be working with this loser?"

After nodding, the operative named Rex said, "Porter is also inclined to be tender-hearted. He's what you might term plus-unruthless."

"I know the type. I suppose he falls in love at the drop of a painted eyelid, eh?"

"You've got it, Stan. And his training scores were dismal.

We can start worrying if he's brought in on this caper. Even though the three of us won't be working side by side, he could still cause us problems."

Stan said, "There have to be more plusses, surely. No? Well, how's his boozing arm?"

"Weak. Three drinks and he gets the giggles."

The heat on Apple's chest began to rise. He tried to concentrate on the film, which, having left the fairground, had been crashing and flashing through that New York street scene.

Apple seemed to be winning with his cling to the visual. He gasped in relief, at which precise moment all noise ended: the screen was showing the silent park shot. Apple's gasp hissed for attention. The men turned and saw him.

Apple walked steadily on over the hot coals. His hands were tied behind, a neck-halter held fore and aft prevented him from moving in haste, and his turban was slipping down over one eye. His feet were bare.

Apple's blush having rushed into full roast, scorching his face and neck, he had immediately started to imagine a market in India. Under a blazing noonday sun, surrounded by a jabbering crowd, he was being forced to perform the hot-coals walk.

This vision was the latest in a long file of "cures," most of which Apple had bought through advertisements in periodicals, all of which had lost their power in time due to familiarity.

"Magic Fakir, the Ancient Remedy that has been Passed Down by the Holy Sages of India," received in a plain envelope, stressed that the vision's heat and fear would shame any blush into retreat.

The bit with a slipping turban Apple had added himself, for piquancy. From the trade name he had been vaguely expecting something of an erotic nature.

Tramping through the smoke, Apple felt himself cooling off. The blush continued to recede. He sighed and opened his eyes, which he had closed in creating the vision.

The two operatives were still looking at him, turned around in their seats. Apple knew from experience that, although he seemed to have been in India for many long minutes, only a few seconds had actually passed since he had gone there.

"That's better," Apple said. "Now I can see." While the men slowly exchanged a glance, he explained that he had just come in that very moment and had done the old trick, they knew the one, of course, everybody did, of closing the eyes for a quick count of ten so that when they were open again the darkness would be lightened.

"Before that," he added, "I didn't even know there were other people in here. It was black and silent." He nodded assuringly. "I couldn't see or hear a thing."

The two men got up. They stepped into the aisle and came back. Their movements were lazy, which, Apple knew, meant that he had fooled them about the tenure of his presence.

Around thirty years old, the desired height of a shade under six feet, the operatives were plainly dressed to go with faces that were in no way out of the ordinary. Rex had fair hair, Stan was dark and wore a moustache.

Coming to a casual halt nearby, they introduced themselves by giving their first names. Nobody offered to shake hands. For one thing, a cool style was always the aim; for another, espionage agents, like undersized people, are not overfond of being touched.

As they would be meeting again shortly, according to Rex, the talk was kept brief, as well as safe: what a pleasant summer Britain was enjoying, with some sunshine almost every day.

The agents left the projection-room. Not once had their expressions even faintly given away that not only did they know of this tall man, but that they had just finished tearing him apart. They were pros.

Apple sat heavily in the nearest armchair. Refusing to dwell in gloom on his own faceless-one status, he stared hard at the screen. Soon he was involved.

The film-clips, all shot covertly from stationary hiding places or moving vehicles, were formed in a continuous circle, without start or finish: Amsterdam, dinner-table, fairground, New York street, park, Amsterdam . . .

Taking about six minutes to complete itself, the footage was devoted to establishing one man, though that it was the same person was not immediately apparent. He looked different in every shot, while staying the same basic type.

X seemed to be average in build. His face was roundish; its features, what could be seen of them, were nondescript. His hair, brown, ranged from short to collar-long. His age was in the thirty-to-forty-five group. His clothing suited the particular occasion: black tie, jeans, duffle-coat, wind-cheater, lounge suit.

It would have been difficult to categorize X ethnically. In respect of nationality, no clue was offered either by his hairstyles or the cut and colour of his clothes. And in the shot of him at table, which (the way he handled knife and fork) might at least have told whether he was North American or European, he was using a spoon on soup.

Apple didn't try for categories. Nor did he try to make any clearer the blurred and innocuous features. He concentrated on studying X's walk, manner, movement of hands, angle of head. But since these were almost as bland as the face, he garnered little through present observation. They would have to be thoroughly absorbed before they came to represent a personality and to be more valuable than physical characteristics, which could be changed, disguised: bulk with padding, height with lifts and headgear, face with contortions or added poundage.

Apple absorbed. Dinner table, fairground, New York street, park, Amsterdam, dinner table, fairground . . .

After a while Apple belched. It happened when he was watching X eat his candy-floss at the fairground. He belched again as the dining scene came on. Patting his stomach, he winced away from recalling what he had learned in Training Four about the torture value in repetition.

Despite himself, his desire to absorb, Apple was beginning to look away from the screen, if only for short periods, when he was saved from further punishment.

The door opened, light flushing Apple into a comforting reality. In leaned the man who had admitted him to the house. He said, "When you've had enough, maybe you'd care to join the others in the room across this hall." The first word of his statement was pronounced with a subtle weight, thus changing the suggestion into something like an order.

The man took the light away. After a final look at the screen, where the now-hateful X had just appeared from the house in Amsterdam, Apple got up to leave. The belch he released at the screen was victorious in nature.

The room, smelling of dust, was dominated by a tall, bright window of frosted glass. Facing it were three chairs, on two of which sat Stan and Rex. Between men and window stood a desk complete with swivel chair. There was nothing else in the room save a calendar that was ten years old.

Sensing the quiet seething that was emanating from the pair of operatives, who sat facing front with arms folded, Apple blinked an unseen apology for the delay as he took the vacant seat.

A door opened. In came Angus Watkin. His entrance was as

dramatic as dandruff. He sat in the swivel chair with a lazy "Good morning, gentlemen."

Sounding like schoolboys who were about to deny everything, the three underlings chorused a reply. Apple joined the others in folding his arms. What was good enough for a pro . . .

Angus Watkin looked down at his hands, which he had placed one on top of the other, like empty gloves. Their owner himself appeared to be similarly void of animation. He was a dull person. Everything about him from hair to clothing was bland, spiritless and middle-of-the-road. His eyes reflected no measure of intelligence above the average. Spymaster Angus Watkin was that middle-aged man who generally gets left out when witnesses list others who had been at the scene.

Looking up, he said, "The man you have been absorbing is known as Clever Freddy. We shall so term him also. He is a free lance espionage agent, dealing in both the political and industrial varieties. He is loyal only to gold."

A second after he had given his tut of disapproval, Apple wished he hadn't: Stan and Rex had made no response. But he didn't care strongly. He was thinking Mission.

"How tall is Clever Freddy?" Angus Watkin asked unexpectedly. As he had looked down, there was no way to indicate at whom the question was aimed.

Apple and the other men answered at roughly the same time. Apple said, "About five ten." The others both said, "Five eight." Apple knew he was right, or righter. He knew how cut and pattern and colour of clothing could blur the true height. He knew all about that art. He had spent a lifetime practicing it.

Angus Watkin said, "Clever Freddy is five feet eight and three-quarter inches tall."

Rather than feel defeated, Apple felt armed. In this matter he knew more than Upstairs. The height could only have been taken by visual measurements—how it related to nearby people or objects.

Keeping his gaze down on the dead pink gloves, Angus Watkin asked other unaimed questions in respect of Clever Freddy's appearance. Apple and his colleagues answered in much the same fashion.

"Now let us go to Scotland," Angus Watkin said. "To an area of the Highlands. To a private estate there called Glengael. Nearby is a small town of almost that same name, Glengaelgow. Any of this familiar to anyone?"

The three men unisoned, "No, sir."

"Excellent," their Control said. He put his hands to the trouble of forming a clasp. "You will now join a small number of people in knowing that on Glengael, which covers thousands of uncultivated acres, there is a secret laboratory. I doubt very much if anyone connected with the estate is aware of its presence."

Apple, feeling flattered at being entrusted with a Most Hush, was unaware of giving his chief a nod of encouragement.

Watkin said, "What, exactly, the laboratory labours at I have no idea. Nor do I know its precise location. That is in the ken of an even smaller number of people. The place is no doubt underground, with access probably through a cave, or something original like that."

An experienced Watkin-watcher, Apple knew that his Control was being scathing about whichever rival department it was who held the responsibility of security and camouflage at the government laboratory.

"Everything, curiously enough, has run smoothly and secretly for quite some time," Angus Watkin said. "But in a matter of days the area is going to be visited by an alien element. Hollywood, so to speak, is stopping by for a few weeks."

"A film unit, sir?" Rex asked.

"Quite. An Anglo-American production company. They'll be shooting exteriors for a feature film. An expensive affair, I understand. Its title escapes me at the moment."

Apple, a film buff, had read of the project in with other filmdom activities. He said, *"My Candle Burns,* sir."

Watkin looked at him. "Thank you."

"It's about Robert Burns, sir. That's the Scottish poet."

"Ah yes."

"Interiors to be shot in London. Director and male lead, Daniel Range. Female lead, Miranda Wheldon."

"Anything else, Porter?"

"No, sir. Sorry."

Watkin murmured, "Oh?" He left that and tapped his clasped hands on the desk three times. "The film unit consists of about eighty people, counting both those in front of the camera and those behind it. Some will stay at a guest-house near the location. Some will stay ten miles away in a hotel in town. The lady star and her entourage will stay at a nearby mansion."

Apple began to see the arrangement. Three concentrations of outsiders, three agents to act as watchdogs.

"The location," Angus Watkin continued, "is on the Glengael estate itself, of course. Permission was granted to the film people only because of the subject matter. The estate's owners are tied in with one of those Burns societies. Permission couldn't be avoided."

The slight drop in his voice for the final sentence Apple translated as meaning *I* could have done so. Which nuance wasn't missed by the other two men, Apple realised with annoyance when they joined him in shuffling a show of appreciation. To exacerbate that, their degree of toady was less pronounced than his own. But he didn't really care. He was thinking Mission.

"There is a proviso to the right of trespass," Angus Watkin

said. "Which is that the film people refrain from straying away from the vicinity of their work. It seems there are protected species of wildlife on the estate, though it isn't a sanctuary in the strict sense."

The agent called Rex said easily, "Handy keep-off sign for the laboratory, sir."

While Angus Watkin was nodding an accord, Apple was wondering why he couldn't come out with casual lines like that.

"All of this wouldn't have been too awkward," Watkin said. "But then word was received somewhere that a freebooter spy was going to be nosing around Glengael at the same time. Obviously, he suspects that something interesting and saleable as information is going on in that region."

After clearing his throat, as if as a form of permission to speak, Stan asked, "Enter Clever Freddy, sir?"

"Enter that same," Angus Watkin said. "The received word, by the way, is pure. It comes from one of Freddy's rivals, who has the same suspicion but happens to be British and loyal."

Rex said, "One assumes, sir, that it's too late now for a calling-off tactic."

"I'm afraid so. Any excuse at all to stop the film people going there would only serve to convince Clever Freddy that what he suspects is true. He is not a fool. In fact, he's quite the reverse. He is further assisted by having the cheek of the Devil, being polylingual, a good actor, and an excellent mimic."

"Also, sir," Rex said, "having no bosses to answer to, he can take wild chances."

Watkin nodded. "On the other hand, a drawback, he has no organization behind him, so that, for instance, it's either difficult or impossible for him to check on the covers of others. You people will be solid in that respect."

Stan said, "So this is a find-the-spook caper, sir."

Apple was glad he hadn't said that, not in those words:

Angus Watkin hated slang. But, because he was thinking Mission, Apple wasn't overly glad; nor, next, overly disappointed when his Control let the slip go by with only a cool glance; nor, after that, overly ashamed of himself—at wanting his colleague to be castigated.

Rex asked, "Clever Freddy isn't British, sir?"

"No, though he did have a half-English mother. The rest of the mixture is Polish, French-Canadian, Italian, and Dutch, and he was reputedly born on a Norwegian cruise ship while it was calling in at Rio de Janeiro."

Angus Watkin unclasped the pink gloves and lay them flat again. "But I was talking of cover, I believe. Your own. These and related matters I shall discuss with you one at a time." He nodded at Rex. "Starting with you."

How Angus Watkin came to be riding in Ethel was straightforward enough, though Apple still found it strange, more so as his chief wasn't sitting regally on the back seat but perched on the pull-down seat behind the driver.

Apple had had no qualms over letting Angus Watkin see his form of transportation. As with every other aspect of his underling's life, Watkin knew about his acquisition and repainting of the notorious Ethel after she had been retired from her life of service as an undercover vehicle, much of which time had been with Upstairs.

Apple, last in line, had only just been ushered back into the interview room when the houseman had entered to remind of an appointment.

"Damn," Angus Watkin had said. He might as well have been saying "Good" for all that his voice and manner gave away. He had got up with, "All right, Porter. I'll talk to you as we share a cab. I have to be elsewhere shortly."

Apple, rising: "I have my car outside, sir."

Now Apple steered into a stream of traffic. That done, he

swiftly returned his head to its sideways position. He didn't want to miss any of what would be coming from Angus Watkin through the open glass panel.

One eye on the road, he asked, "You were saying, sir?"

"I wasn't, Porter. But I will be, from here on, beginning with the fact that you were chosen for possible use on this little errand because of a possession of yours."

"Really, sir?"

"Really," Angus Watkin said. "You have, I understand, a dog of a certain breed. An Ibizan hound."

"Yes, sir, I do."

"That is the possession in question."

Apple was too intrigued to feel slighted that it wasn't some personal quality that was being called into use. He said calmly, "I see, sir."

"You do not, of course," Watkin said. "But you will when I tell you that, although the original script called for one particular breed of dog to appear in the film, we're hoping to have that changed to an Ibizenco."

Apple hazarded, "In which case, sir, my cover will be that I'm the dog's trainer and handler."

"Well done. Please pay a little attention to the road."

Fully facing front with a jerk, Apple straightened Ethel out and reduced speed. He was more stimulated than he had been all through a stimulating morning. Could it be, he thought, that he and Monico were going to be working on a caper together?

Apple's dog, of a breed that was peculiar to the island of Ibiza, looked like a gingery greyhound whose coat had been brushed the wrong way. A quiet, self-effacing animal who rarely barked and who had given up cats, Monico lodged at a farm that was near his master's weekend cottage.

Turning his head back to the side, Apple said worriedly, "I

doubt very much, sir, if an Ibizan hound was ever seen in Burns country."

"I doubt if the original breed was either. It's a chow. But that, as I am informed they say, is show business."

"They do, sir, yes, say that."

"But to get on," Angus Watkin pursued, "if all goes well on the change of dog, you, with some thirty others, will be staying in the guest-house. It's normally used only by hunting and shooting people, but is empty at this time of year, between seasons."

Absently: "Well done, sir."

"Every day you will go with the actors and technicians out to the filming location. It's a few minutes as the car drives from the guest-house. Thus you'll always be on hand where the people are concentrated, which is where Clever Freddy is most likely to be." After naming the ranks of location personnel, he asked, "Know anything about such matters, Porter?"

"No, sir," Apple said. He might have done better, lied, if it hadn't been that his neck was beginning to ache, which had also stopped him from dwelling pleasantly on the fact that here he was, driving along in Ethel with a spymaster behind him whispering crisp orders.

After giving his head a quick flick away and back, Apple said, "We could always say it was my first movie job."

"No, Porter," Angus Watkin said lazily. "That's exactly the kind of thing Clever Freddy will be on the watch for—an outsider. He will, of course, be sensitive to the possibility of a counterspy being there."

Affably: "Of course."

"You will be put through a crash course at Damian House on film-making operations, as well as told about the other pictures you have worked on with the animal. What, incidentally, is the creature's name?"

Being aware that his Control knew Monico's name perfectly

well, Apple turned front to mumble "Portico." When Watkin said "Yes, to be sure, Monico," Apple felt soothed in neck and soul.

"And can Monico obey simple orders?" Angus Watkin went on. "Sit, come, walk?"

Apple flicked his head and said, as if faintly offended, "Yes, sir." The lie was so outrageous that he found it easy to make, like asking for the impossible.

"It doesn't matter," his Control said in the manner of a deaf man. "At Damian House your animal will receive training in obedience, just as you will be told what a dog-trainer's life entails. You will also be given the usual cover documents, as well as a car."

"But I already have a car, sir."

There was a pause before Angus Watkin said, "And that concludes what I have to tell you, Porter. You may let me off at the next set of traffic lights, if you please."

"Yes, sir," Apple said. He took the silent news with satisfaction—of a subtle form. To not only be given a caper, but to have both Monico *and* Ethel in on it, that was a perfection which would have made him apprehensive.

Facing front, neck happy, Apple drove with both eyes on the road and kept a watch on his Control via glances in the rear-view mirror.

Despite his simmer of excitement, Apple couldn't help but notice the way Angus Watkin was looking around at Ethel's interior. Which made him wonder if his chief had arranged that reminder of an appointment in order to get a ride in the ex-taxi-cab.

Possibly, Apple thought. It wouldn't have been simply a question of not wanting to ask; it was also an opportunity for real-life practice in playing with people and situations. Angus Watkin's ploys frequently had a double edge.

Apple wondered, therefore, if Watkin was recalling Ethel's

and his own past, the espionage adventures they had shared when they were younger.

But Apple realised that his high spirits were causing him to think foolishly. Angus Watkin lacked the necessary sentiment, being only part-human. As his professional mind never rested, he was probably judging how many unconscious KGB agents he could fit into the vehicle.

Apple drew into the side of the road to double-park. Angus Watkin got out. In doing so, he glanced at his watch. Before closing the door he said, "You and your animal are expected at Damian House for lunch. Goodbye."

Driving off in a dither, Apple came close to thinking, Wait till I tell Monico.

"See, lad, most Anglo-Saxons treat their dogs like children. All that spoiling and special foods, all that diddems-den and oochi-coochi. It's not surprising their poor pets is neurotic. See, the bewildered creature don't know if it's a dog or a child. It's insecure. You get me?"

"Yes, Mr. Ackroyd."

"The best thing you can do for a dog is treat it like an animal. Then it knows where it is. It'll respect you all the more and be as happy as moonbeams."

Ackroyd nodded. He was a serious-faced, no-nonsense Yorkshireman of around seventy, with a short, stout body and skinny limbs. The few stray hairs on his head were white. He had sat at Apple's table after lunch with, "Call me Mr. Ackroyd, lad. I'm in the canine game. What I don't know about that species ain't worth knowing."

Now he said, "Ideally, a dog should live in the country, sleep outdoors, get fed once a day, and have plenty of work to do. The happiest dogs of all belong to sheep-farmers."

Apple bragged, "Monico lives on a farm during the week."

"Good. And with him being a foreigner, like, without your

domestic type's centuries of coddling in his blood, he might not be too daft—even if he is a gazehound. If you know what that is."

"They're the ones who hunt by sight rather than scent. They're believed to be less intelligent than other breeds."

"And rightly believed," Ackroyd said. "But, look, have you trained him to do anything at all?"

Apple told proudly of how, when Monico lived with him in his Bloomsbury flat, where there was a no-pets rule, he used to sneak him in and out of the building by having him wait upstairs until he heard from below the all-clear signal.

"A good sign," Ackroyd said. "But we don't have all the time in the world to work with him. In fact, it'd be a good idea if we got started right away."

They got up and left the dining-room, where about a dozen people were still lingering over the meal.

Damian House was a handsome mansion set in ample grounds. With all the attributes of a luxury hotel, from tennis courts to nine-hole golf course, it passed in the neighbourhood as a holiday home for armed services personnel. Hidden from casual view were the giveaway attributes such as obstacle course, shooting range and a wealth of sophisticated radio equipment.

With Monico running on ahead tentatively, Apple and Ackroyd walked away from the house. Soon they came to an open space surrounded by trees.

"Stand back and watch, lad," the Yorkshireman said. "I'll bring you in on it presently. And don't say a word."

"No, sir," Apple said nervously. He felt like a father at a school play.

Ackroyd put a leash on Monico and from a bulging pocket of his tweed jacket produced a biscuit. He lay it down on the grass, let Monico sniff it, then jerked him away with a sharp negative accompanied by an upraised forefinger. He walked

Monico a short way off and said, "Sit." This normal-tone command he accompanied with a down-pushing gesture.

Monico went on standing. He looked at Apple as if wondering where he had seen him before.

By shoving down on the hind quarters, Ackroyd got Monico to sit. After a pause he pointed flat-handed toward the biscuit while saying a cosy, "Yes." He led Monico back there. The dog sniffed the biscuit briefly before turning away with disinterest.

"Sorry," Apple said. "He only likes the sweet kind."

With no hint of impatience or disgust, Ackroyd asked, "So which one of us is going to go back and get some?"

When Apple returned with a bag of small sugar-buns, all that the kitchen had to offer, the Yorkshireman started again. This time, the routine having been noted by Apple, he was asked to stay at Ackroyd's side while copying his actions and commands as near to simultaneously as possible.

It was fifteen minutes before Monico reacted to the voice/gesture command not to eat, rather than being stopped from doing so by the leash; thirty minutes before he would sit without being pushed down; one minute before he got the message that the bun was his for the taking.

After he had gone through the routine several times minus the leash, he was taken through it again by Apple alone. They both performed immaculately.

"A fairly good start," Ackroyd said. "And, see, he'll always associate signals with something good—food."

"Brilliant," Apple said, stooping to give Monico a pat.

"Never pet a dog excessively, lad. Makes 'em soft."

Straightening: "Sorry, Mr. Ackroyd."

The old man rubbed his hands together. "Right. So let's have you continue with the same piece of business. But from now on, I want you to lower your voice a bit each time. Then cut it off altogether. See, we'll have Monico doing it on hand-signals alone."

That came to pass after nearly an hour and a half and after Apple had cheated occasionally in the latter stages by whispering the words he had stopped using. Ackroyd expressed satisfaction.

He said, "Here endeth the first lesson." A minute later, as they were strolling back, he confided, "I always say that."

There were many more lessons, a two-hour period every morning, afternoon and evening. The last were held indoors, in the lounge, where Monico grew accustomed to working among people and noise, and, in particular, to being under the strong lights that had been set up. He made progress in fits and starts.

Ackroyd never showed impatience. He never smiled either, but his manner was friendly in a bluff way. He quickly won Monico's affection. Apple told himself he wasn't jealous.

Meanwhile, there were other matters to be seen to. One day Apple had a long conversation with a tipsy man who seemed to know all about animals in movies. Between sips of port, Apple absorbing, he talked of Lassie, Trigger, Rin Tin Tin, Cheetah, Silver, Francis. He also gave full details on the two films that Apple and Monico had made in South Africa last year.

It was on leaving this session that Apple saw Stan. The agent, whose dark moustache had been trimmed shorter, was coming out of the dining room.

"Hi," Apple said. "Just arrived?"

As icy as any resort guest in danger of being upstaged, Stan said, "As a matter of fact, I was here before you."

Quickly: "I was here ten years ago."

"So was I."

Cautiously: "I came in May."

The agent said, "I have to be moving. Things to do. See you."

Several times Apple had lectures on movie-making techniques, jargon and protocol. The lecturer was a hefty matron with every illusion intact, including the one that she had a petite form. She poured out her love of the eighth lively art while showing photographs of equipment.

Among scores of other items, Apple learned that the best boy wasn't an angelic apprentice or the juvenile lead, but the man who operated the dolly, which wasn't a toy but a wheeled contraption used for moving the camera; that the gaffer was no old codger but the chief electrician; that the boom wasn't a noise but a microphone-rod; that the grip wasn't a hold but a man who moved things around.

Apple was fascinated. He absorbed with the greatest of ease. His only hope was that all this wouldn't spoil his enjoyment of the finished products.

Apple didn't see Stan again, but did catch sight of Rex, twice. The fair-haired operative was striding around the grounds like a robot.

One afternoon Apple was shown the cover documents he would use if his part in the caper went ahead. He saw that he would be Tim Gordon, bachelor, thirty, ex-army dog-handler, of Bromley, Kent.

Next, the same brisk young man took Apple out to the garage and showed him his car—a small Austin van with TIM'S KENNELS painted poorly on the sides—while describing what it was like to run a training school for dogs, between getting the occasional handler job in pictures.

Returning to his room one evening, Apple found that a copy of *My Candle Burns* had been delivered. Some of the screenplay's pages were yellow. These proved on examination to be the ones on which the dog-actor appeared. Apple read them with care.

The yellow-page action, covering several months in the film story, all took place on the same village street. Mostly, the dog was seen at the heels of his movie master. He also had solo shots which called for no great acting gifts. Apple felt less worried about Monico being able to cope.

He read the whole screen-play. It concerned an episode in the poet's life when he was pursued by the vengeful menfolk of three girls he had seduced. The most persistent was a laird with a taste for exotic canines. He and the hero fought a duel at the end. Although no Robert Burns expert, Apple knew that, at best, the story was an exaggeration—except as regards the seductions, which had been limited in number for the sake of credibility.

By the fifth morning Monico could obey ten different commands, though not consistently. He was apt to do the opposite or begin to stroll off.

"That's all right," Ackroyd said. "A few more days and he'll be a different animal."

But that was to be the last lesson. A staff member came with a note: the change in breeds having been accepted, Apple had to leave for Scotland at once.

While Apple glittered, the old man bent to fondle Monico's ears. He said, "He'll soon forget me." Straightening, he added, "I always say that."

TWO

It was dusk when Apple arrived, after eight hours of fast driving. The guest-house, built without frills from hand-hewn stone, stood alone beside a winding secondary road. Blancairn looked attractive and inviting with many of its windows lit, an urban oasis in a landscape of rocks and pines.

After parking at the side of the house among a score of other vehicles, including a bus, Apple carried his bag inside. Monico quickly followed. Despite the date, the evening air was chill.

Oak beams, copperware, saggy furniture dressed in chintz, a log fire burning in a massive hearth—the lobby was as inviting as the facade. People were moving and sitting. Their casual clothes pleased Apple, who had dressed in slacks and a sweater.

The woman who intercepted Apple on his way to the desk said, "Hey, I never saw a dog like that before."

"Well, I never saw a wig like that before."

"I've got ten. All different colours."

"I've only got one dog, and he never changes," Apple said. "Hello. I'm Tim Gordon."

She was Cookie, a plump-nearing American in her late thirties. Her jeans and denim shirt were ill-complemented by ornate spectacles, heavy cosmetics and a green wig.

In explaining about Monico, Apple explained himself. With a cheery-raucous call, Cookie introduced him to the others who were manning the lobby. They waved. Apple smiled, politely but without professional interest. He had already established that no one here could be Clever Freddy.

Cookie, still fussing over Monico, went with Apple to the desk. It was cowed by a spinsteresque woman whose eyebrows spelt "Proprietress." Signing in meekly, Apple was relieved to learn that it had previously been arranged that Monico would sleep in his room.

As they moved toward the stairs, Cookie said that shooting had been going on for two days, and there would be ten or fifteen or thirty more. "Depends on the weather. In this neck of the woods, hell, anything can happen."

They went on talking shop. Cookie was about to drift away at the stairs, but Apple kept the talk going. She was pleasant, she seemed to know everything, she might come in useful.

Wincing at himself for that, yet because of it feeling the hardened, cynical pro, Apple asked, "And what's your game?"

"Driver. I bus you people out to the location and back, as well as whatever other driving's needed. But it wasn't always thus, as they say in the movies. I used to be a stunt person."

"You don't look that hard."

"Seems I wasn't," Cookie said. "The wall was harder. And that was the end of my stunting. You've probably noticed the limp."

"Can't say I have," Apple lied.

Cookie grinned up at him with "Thanks."

Another female voice said, "I *beg* your pardon."

Apple looked the other way. He got a shock. Not only was he being looked down on by a woman, but that woman was stunningly beautiful. He then saw that, although the latter was quite true, the former was so only because she was standing on the stairs.

"Hello, Velma," Cookie said drily. "Meet Tim."

Velma, who was blonde, slim and dressed in an evening

gown, gave Apple an up-down with her magnificent eyes. "Hello," she lazed. *"If* I may get by?"

While Apple, unmoving, still slightly in shock, was trying to think of something witty and attention-getting to say, Cookie told the blonde how he fitted into the picture-making.

Velma sighed. She brushed sinuously past Apple with a deadpan "How utterly fascinating."

Apple turned to watch her go. "She's fabulous," he mumbled. "Must be a new superstar."

"Velma Wilde," Cookie said, "plays a maid in this flick. It's her best part yet, though she never gets to say a word."

Apple's awe was undiminished. He watched the cool beauty until she went into the bar. When, sighing himself alert, he glanced around, Cookie had gone.

In his room under the eaves Apple found a plaid-blanket bed for Monico, a note from the producer bidding him welcome, and an official copy of the screen-play.

He sat on the bed to glance through the script, look for changes, then lay down to ease the numbness of his eight-hour-sit buttocks. He fell asleep. Awake again an hour later, he had a quick wash and went downstairs.

In a deserted dining-room an old waiter told him accusingly that supper was over. "But we can do you a wee plate of cold cuts, sir, if you're inclined to suchlike."

"Wonderful," Apple said. "And if you could fix something for my friend here."

"Aye, that's arranged."

"But tell me, you don't manage this dining-room all by yourself, do you?"

The question, right in its tone of sympathy as well as subject, elicited eventually, before the waiter left, what Apple really wanted to know. Of Blancairn's seven staff members, male and female, only one was under sixty and of recent employment: McKay, a gardener, about thirty-five, had been here a week.

Humming, Apple sat down. To show that he knew nothing whatever about espionage, he sat not with his back to a wall and in sight of the door, but smack in the middle of the room and facing a window.

The old waiter returned with two plates. Monico's princely scraps lasted a matter of seconds. Apple took longer over his meal, which included home-baked bread dusted with wheat germ. He was still eating, and beginning to feel cheated that the quirkiness of life hadn't offered anything through the window other than darkness, when Monico gave a gasp of warning. Apple looked around.

The man who had come in, who strode over and introduced himself as Arthur Reed, production manager, wore a smart lounge suit and a bow-tie. Average in build, he had a boyish face framed by a mass of auburn, professionally dressed hair. His manner was Rising Executive, as smooth and quick as an UP elevator, and just as mechanical. His accent was mid-Atlantic.

Apple was told that his arrival had been eagerly awaited, asked if this was the old fellow, was it, begged to ask for whatever he desired, and assured that everything was going to be Fine, Super, Great.

Arthur Reed finished his plastic speech with, "You can always come to me with a problem. I'm currently at the King's Messenger, a hotel in town."

"Check," Apple said efficiently. "And when do we start to work, Mr. Reed?"

"Arthur, please," the production manager said. Briefly, he rounded his eyes: Sincerity. "You start in the morning, Tim. There's an eight o'clock call. The bus will be at the door. Out at the location an assistant director will show you what's required for the day's shots. You'll have ample time to rehearse the old fellow."

"Monico, please."

"Right—Monico. He's going to be just super."

Apple said, "You have it all at your fingertips, Arthur. I really appreciate that. You must've been in this business from the cradle."

"Television mostly. This is my first feature movie. And it looks like being a fine one."

He went on to talk about the film project, making it sound slightly less sacred than a pilgrimage to Mecca. Finally, he put a forefinger on his watch, though he didn't look at its dial.

"I mustn't keep you," he said. "But before I go—any questions?" He shook his head.

"Well," Apple said, "will Monico be working every day?"

"Looks like it, Tim. In any case, you'll get a call-sheet the evening before. Everybody does. You'll probably find that one's been slipped under your door now. But I mustn't interrupt your meal any longer."

Alone again, Apple mused pleasurably that Arthur Reed, in addition to being Clever Freddy material in build and age, was almost a caricature of filmdom's executive type. In fact, wasn't that bow-tie carrying things a little too far?

After supper Apple lit a cigarette and strolled out to the lobby. Dogs being a form of introduction bureau, as the shy and the lonely well know, he was quickly in conversation with some of the lobbyers. In the main, they were different from those who had been there earlier. But there was still no one of the right material. Apple didn't mind. He was in no hurry whatever.

Presently, Apple went into the bar. On a stool at one end sat Velma Wilde. She was the only person present who wasn't either smiling or talking. Apple thought she looked sensational. When her gaze caught his, he smiled. In looking away the bit player made her eyelids heavy.

Apple gave himself a point anyway, for daring to try. He turned the other way, saw Cookie at a table with a group of men, went across and asked, "May I join you?"

He was made welcome. More so when he suggested that he buy a round of drinks. Soon, sherry on the rocks in hand, he was part of a discussion about the original *King Kong.* Monico slunk boredly under a nearby table.

As with the other people Apple had met here at Blancairn, the five men were some British, some American. They were electricians and grips. For one physical reason or another, none was of caper interest. Nor, Apple saw, was there anyone else in the bar who could be a prospect. He reminded himself drably that Clever Freddy did not, of course, have to be operating in this area; he could be under the jurisdiction of Stan or Rex.

Not liking that thought, Apple gave his full attention to the talk.

It wandered like a fly on a map, moving from films to diets to athletics, with brief stops on a dozen other topics. Meanwhile, two of the men left. Their places were taken by a couple. The man was sixty.

When another grip left also, Apple moved around to his chair, which was beside Cookie. He drew her into a private conversation while the newcomers complained tipsily how much easier technicians had it than extras.

Apple said, "I met Arthur Reed a while ago. Have you worked with him before?"

"Never even heard of him, honey," Cookie said, giving her navy blue wig a pat. "But I guess he knows what he's doing, even though he talks a lot of bunk."

"He does?"

"Hey, I bet you don't know that bunk's short for bunkum,

which is a version of Buncombe, which was someplace where they made nonsense speeches."

Apple not only knew, he knew that Buncombe was a county in North Carolina. It wasn't easy for him to say "How fascinating."

Cookie nodded absently. "But I think Reed's right in bringing in a bit of security. I sure feel better."

"Security?"

"Out at the location. Reed says that this guy Wilson Croft he hired is to ensure that no one wanders away and disturbs the wildlife. But I know the real reason."

"Oh?" Apple said. "Tell me."

At that moment the female extra began to quote Omar Khayyám. Her friend groaned, the technicians jeered, and Cookie defended that poor Milly had every right to get bombed, since she wasn't on call tomorrow.

Sitting it out, Apple refrained implacably from correcting Milly's variations of the Fitzgerald translation. His toes ached.

This was still going on when Cookie leaned close to Apple with the whisper, "Speak of the devil. Wilson Croft. See? The beaver."

The man whom she indicated by her nod had just come in and moved to the bar. The dense black beard he wore contained more hair than his crew cut. His pants and windcheater, matching green, had a uniform appearance. In height and age Wilson Croft was a prospect.

The curtain came down on Milly's declaiming with the arrival of a tray of drinks. Apple waited until these were sorted out before again claiming Cookie's attention. They bent close in the bar's rising noise.

Apple asked, "So tell me, what's the real reason for Croft being on the set?"

"I think our location's jinxed. Some of the guys agree with

me. I'd say that Reed obviously does. Even though the straying bit is legit, we surely don't need a watch-dog."

The best way to encourage elaboration, as Apple had learned in Training Four, was disagreement. He said, "Oh, I don't know. People become forgetful after a while."

"Hell, we're not a bunch of kids."

"Anyway, jinxing went out with high-buttoned witches."

Cookie shook her head insistently, the light flashing off her rhinestone-clustered spectacles like in a baby ballroom. "This old Scotland is a weird place, Tim. Full of ghosties and ghoulies and stuff like that."

"Even so," Apple said, "you really think there's a jinx on the location?" He was listening carefully while telling himself to get it right: *location* was the place of filming operations, *set* the background against which actors were filmed.

"I guess I do," Cookie said. "Some funny things have happened in the last few days."

"Give me an example."

"That's not easy—except for yesterday. They were little things. A tool missing, a take being spoiled, somebody tripping over a cable. You know. Borderliners."

Apple asked, "What was yesterday's thing?"

Cookie shuffled her plump shoulders with the gossip's jiggle. "One of the prop-men," she said. "He'd moved off and was sitting on a bunch of high rocks. He fell and bruised his leg pretty badly."

"That can happen anywhere, Cookie."

"But the deal is, he swears he was pushed. He felt a hand or whatever on his back, and down he came. Sure, he could be covering for himself—too many nips from the flask—but he could also be telling the truth."

"Of course," Apple said. "But can jinxes supply pushes?"

"Me, I'll believe anything. I even believe movies. It embarrasses me the way I fall apart at the sad ones."

They were interrupted by a burst of shouting from the others at the table: Ms. Extra had got up to do a tap-dance. Apple watched the performance happily. He told himself that the mishaps, if truly non-accidental, meant that Clever Freddy was on the job.

The male extra pulled his companion down into her seat. He looked jealous. The noise resided with the dancer.

Turning to Apple, Cookie said, "As I was saying before, et cetera, et cetera. Listen. It's as though something out there was trying to drive us away."

The reverse, Apple thought, if our Freddy was the jinx. He would want to make the filming, the unit's legitimate presence, last as long as possible, he the while trying to sniff out the laboratory. Mishaps were delayers, not attacks.

He said, "Well, Arthur Reed can't be in agreement with you all the way on this. Otherwise he would've brought in a medicine-man or something, not a flesh-and-blood guard."

"Me, I'll be glad when we get through here and go on to London," Cookie said with a flap of her hand, as though waving the subject goodbye. "Are you in for interiors, Tim?"

They talked shop. As before, Apple looked whenever possible at the bearded security man. As Clever Freddy material, his weave had grown stronger. Who was less suspected of a crime than the patrolling policeman?

At ten-thirty, to Apple's surprise, the bar began to empty. Wilson Croft had already left. Next, Cookie got up. She said, "It's getting late. We have an early call." Apple quickly produced a yawn.

Before going upstairs, he took Monico outside for a run. They went back and forth along the dark, deserted road. The only sound came from Apple's footfalls, the only lights to be seen anywhere belonged to the house. Monico was first to head back inside.

In his room, after reading the call-sheet that he had found on the floor, Apple went straight to bed. Preparing for sleep, he thought of Arthur Reed, Wilson Croft and the new gardener McKay in the hope that his subconscious would dissect the trio while he slept.

What awoke Apple was a scratching sound. It ripped away his dream of being invited to tea Upstairs. Annoyed, he turned over to find that Monico was pawing at the covers. The message: nature calls.

Grumbling at Monico for not having stayed out longer, Apple switched on lights and got up. It was midnight. As he was already in pajamas, plus the heavy socks he always wore away from home to compensate for short beds, dressing was a mere matter of stepping into shoes and putting on an overcoat.

Apple and Monico went downstairs. Although the lobby was deserted, voices were coming from the bar, one of them Ms. Extra's.

Turning back behind the staircase, Apple wended his way through dim passages until he found an exit. He went out onto gravel. Stopping there, he drew the door closed except for a crack, which gave an eke of light to the darkness.

Monico went from the gravel onto grass. He began to sniff about. Apple hissed at him to hurry bloody up. Chill air was striking through his pajama bottoms.

It would be more sensible, Apple decided, to wait inside, instead of standing in the freezing cold. He turned and pushed the door. It went only partway before stopping with a sudden thud.

What had stopped it, Apple saw on trying again immediately (and succeeding, the door going fully open) was the forehead of a man. He was reversing unsteadily along the passage with a hand to his brow.

"Oops," Apple said. "Sorry."

"Kind of you," the man grated. He was British. "Thanks."

"I didn't know you were there, of course. But sorry all the same. Are you hurt badly?"

"No. It's okay."

Apple said, "I'm Tim Gordon, the animal-handler."

The man drew his hand down. "Johnny Fleming. Props."

"You're not the one who fell off a rock, are you?"

Coldly, the man said, "No."

After weighing values, Apple realised that here was the best prospect so far. The prop-man looked so much the ideal espionage agent that he would have made Angus Watkin almost think of smiling.

Apart from the faint red mark worn currently on its forehead, Johnny Fleming's face was bland to the point of obscurity. The hair was equally nondescript. He wore jeans and a black sweater, he was thirty-five to forty, and he stood five feet ten inches tall.

Apple, who was still out on the gravel, moved aside. "Please come through."

Johnny Fleming said, "Thanks, but I've changed my mind." He turned away. "Good night."

"Could I buy you a drink by way of apology?"

"No, thanks," Fleming threw back. He went from sight around a corner.

Apple stood on thoughtfully. He pictured the prop-man on a New York street, in a park, in Amsterdam, at dinner, on a fairground, in New York . . .

Apple tasted bile. He belched.

A voice said mock-reprovingly, "Manners."

Apple turned. Coming over the grass, near where Monico was sampling the bouquet of a tree before deciding whether or not to use it, was the man who had been in the bar earlier, Wilson Croft. His beard and the darkness combined to make it appear, weirdly, as if he had only half a face.

This effect eased when he came closer to the light, crunching to a halt on the gravel. He introduced himself. His Scottish accent was sharp.

"Tim Gordon," Apple said, going across with his hand out. It wasn't so much that he wanted to shake hands, more to get a close look at that beard.

"I saw the wee accident with Fleming," Wilson Croft said. He glanced groundward, as if to make sure that Apple wasn't standing on something.

"If it had happened out on the location, we'd be calling it part of the jinx."

The security man snorted. "So you've heard that bit of nonsense, have you? It's complete rubbish. The story started because an old man was in the lobby here telling about a sacred place where they used to practice the Old Religion. Owner and staff say they've never heard of it."

"Some seem convinced."

"Because they want to be. Film crews often make drama out of a job they're on, especially if it's not particularly interesting. Haven't you found that?"

"Mmmm," Apple mumbled before saying, "but things have been happening out there, apparently."

Wilson Croft shook his head. "Only Bill falling off a rock. I think he was dozing. There's a logical explanation for everything, Mr. Gordon."

"I tend to think so myself, Mr. Croft. Therefore it could well be that Bill was pushed by a rival—another prop-man."

"For what reason?"

"No idea. Promotion. A union business. Personal grudge." Croft smiled. "Trying to play detective?"

"Oh no," Apple said quickly. "Not at all." He called to Monico.

"Anyway, the prop-men all seem to get along well together. Cheery lot. Except for that Fleming one. But he's a stranger to the others."

Apple's caper interest, which had been flagging because of the cold and the beard's look of genuineness, took a turn upward. "He's new on the job?"

"I believe so. We haven't talked. He's not a mixer."

Although Apple put a crown on his choice of Johnny Fleming as suspect number one, he cautioned himself not to ask too many questions—if only for the fact that they encouraged questions in those questioned.

But it was too late, evidently, for Wilson Croft asked, "How long have you been in this line of work, Mr. Gordon?" Like someone settling for a long chat, he folded his arms comfortably.

"Years," Apple said. He exaggerated a shiver. "Must get back to bed. I've just got over a cold. So I'll say good night to you."

"Ah well. Good night. And mind how you go. We don't want any more violence, do we?"

"This is outrageous. You have no right to approach me in the street."

"That's a terrible hat you're wearing."

"A poor excuse, sir. I am a lady alone."

"We all have days like that, kid."

The man and woman, in the clothing of eighteenth-century gentry, stood facing each other on one side of the village street. There was no other side. The cottages and an inn, authentic-looking to the last crack, had been erected recently. The buildings were only skin-deep.

The woman, touching her bonnet with a nervous hand, said, "Please let me pass, sir."

"Got your ID card?"

"No earthly good can come of this foolishness."

"And so on and so forth."

Most of the exteriors of *My Candle Burns* were being shot

without sound; voices and other effects would be dubbed in later. The actor, who was in reverse to the camera, his lip movements thus unseen, was speaking merely to regulate the to-and-fro of an exchange.

Now he bowed. The actress walked head-high past and a voice called, "Cut. We'll print that one." The murmur of talk from around the set rose in volume, two or three people clapped lazily, others began to move about and stretch.

It was sunny noon. Shooting had been going on at a reasonable pace since nine. Apple, long since finished rehearsing with Monico the scenes that would be filmed later, had been free to wander around the location.

The sole dent in his enjoyment had been the fact that neither the female lead nor main supporting actress were here today, but even that was eased by having Velma Wilde to ogle.

In a crescent that spread back untidily from the one-sided village was the paraphernalia of filming: huge camera, lights, sound truck, reflectors, generators, honey wagon (portable toilets), buses and cars and trucks. Then came a temporary corral with horses, a night-watchman's tent, and the long caravans that served as dressing-rooms, office, make-up and wardrobe. Lesser flotsam included folding chairs and personal belongings of the crew. It all looked as efficient and organised as a can of worms.

Apple was getting along well with everyone. He had, he felt, been accepted. This was partly due to his response at the entrance to the estate—a simple gate set in a waist-high wall.

Cookie, the bus driver, had turned to Apple and said, "As this is your first day, I'm going to give you the honour of letting us in."

Not until he had stepped outside did Apple see the gag. Passenger laughter coincided with the smell. It came from a large pigpen which lay fifty yards off, beyond the gate. Apple had hammed up deep breathing and called out that there was nothing like fresh country air. On returning to the bus, gate seen to, he had received a round of applause for being a good sport.

Apple had also established friendly relations with the group who had come from the hotel in town, mostly bit players and wardrobe people but headed by the actor-director. Daniel Range was a burly, hawk-faced man of fifty who had time only for a fast handshake.

Apple, in fact, had been received well by everyone except Johnny Fleming. Twice the bland prop-man, seeing Apple's approach, had made himself scarce. However, Apple was certain that neither Fleming nor Wilson Croft had been absent from the location for any significant period.

Apple had seen no one new to add to his list of suspects. He thought it would probably remain at Arthur Reed, gardener McKay, Croft and Fleming. The smaller the better.

Apple now headed for the set on noting something of interest: one of the prop-men who was helping roll a cart into position had a limp.

Apple's interest increased when he saw that he was about to pass near where Velma Wilde was lounging, which was as near to Daniel Range as she could get without seeming to be picking his pocket.

But Apple went back to thinking Mission when his searching smile was stared at by the bit player as though it were a dentist's bill.

The prop-men were soon finished. They ambled off looking tired, as if their union had won them that right and they were determined to exercise it. Apple followed.

He got the limping man alone when he sat on a truck bumper. He was a lean cockney of forty with an expansive stretch of baldness. Apple remembered seeing Bill in the lobby last night.

Monico was the subject at first. Next Apple asked about the

accident. Bill said it wasn't, nor was it what some were insinuating.

"Which is that I'm lying to cover up on account of I wouldn't got no insurance money if it was me own fault."

"I don't think that," Apple soothed. "Not that I go for the jinx idea either."

"I'm with you there. Don't believe in all that weird stuff, me. And it was definitely flesh and blood as give me a shove."

Apple got out and offered cigarettes. He was avoiding dwelling on what had only just occurred to him—that it could be the laboratory people who were responsible for the location incidents, in hopes of driving the crew away.

When the cigarettes were alight, Apple asked, "Who would want to hurt you, Bill?"

"Gawd knows, mate. Could even've been meant as a joke."

"Where was our security man when it happened?"

"Croft? Didn't see him till afterwards. Probably, he was loitering around the outskirts here. That's an easy job, if you like."

"Arthur Reed seems to think it's necessary."

"Rubbish," the prop-man said. "I had meself a wander away yesterday, exercise this leg, and not only did I not get stopped, I saw two others out there."

It was at that moment that the explosion happened.

Although short, the noise was loud enough to halt all talk and action. Everyone looked toward the source, at the location's rear. The silence lasted three seconds. Then came shouts, a scream, and a sound like distant thunder.

Apple shot up from his sit on the bumper. His height allowed him to see over various pieces of equipment. What he saw was a dozen horses. Having broken out of their corral, they were charging this way.

"Stampede!" Apple shouted. That was what others were yelling, as well as shorter words.

The human hubbub and animal thundering increased. People either ran, circling and leaping obstacles, or they climbed onto the bigger ones. Some people from far back were running forward to see. The horses gave shrill whinnies as they came.

A reflector-stand crashed over. Clapper boy beat best boy onto a stack of boxes. An actor ran inside an open doorway of the village tavern.

Velma Wilde, giving a pretty squeal, flung herself into the arms of Daniel Range, who immediately flung her at an assistant director, who dodged. Velma fell to the ground with a raucous scream.

Threading between the flotsam and equipment, the horses were galloping in separate groups of three or four. They tossed their heads, rolled their eyes.

The explosion was responsible for the stampede, Apple and Bill agreed as they stood erect from their fast climb onto the truck's front. Monico had long since been underneath.

One group of horses, changing course, headed for the truck.

Apple gasped. Nearby, there was no one left below apart from Velma Wilde. She was still lying on the ground and crosswise on the path that the horses were taking. Apple gasped because this was an eighteen-carat opportunity.

Almost before he had decided to act, he was doing so. He leapt far out from the truck, chased by Bill's cry of surprise. Landing well, he covered the remaining yards at top speed, chased now by the horses.

Velma Wilde, propped motionless on one elbow, was staring this way with her eyes looking as roundly large as her mouth, which was giving out a yell.

After a final stride Apple threw himself downward with a side-turning swing. He landed half on top of the bit player and half beside her. The latter became three-quarters as Velma dropped back in answer to a hissed "Lie flat!"

The horses were here.

Dust flew and hooves thundered, nostrils snorted and the ground trembled. Cheek to cheek, body to body, Apple held lustfully tight to Velma Wilde as the horses jumped over them one at a time.

The breeze left, hoofbeats faded.

Apple and the girl lay still. They went on doing so until the most prominent sounds were nervous laughter and shouts with a panic-over resonance. Apple was having a fine time.

Velma said, "Do you mind?" She added as they began to get up, "Thank you."

"I suppose we're lucky to be alive," Apple said, trying to look harassed while at the same time looking brave.

"Yes. We're lucky."

"Are you all right?"

"Perfectly, thank you," the bit player said, cool. She stood beside him and looked up. "What's your name?" Told, she thanked him again and walked on.

Apple warned himself against being disappointed. Anything could happen from here on, once Velma got it into her head that he was her gallant rescuer, and so long as she didn't find out that no horse will ever willingly step on a human being.

It was two hours before filming resumed. First, everyone had to tell everyone else about his own experience, including what he had been doing when, as well as discuss the whole matter at length.

The emotional atmosphere was cheerful. Most agreed that they were fortunate: no one was even scratched and damage to equipment was minimal, whereas injury could have been severe, if not fatal, and shooting could have been postponed for days.

There was some talk of jinx, particularly from Cookie ("I was dozing in the bus when . . ."), but scoffed at by Daniel Range ("I'd just decided to shoot when . . ."), and outright dismissed by security man Wilson Croft ("I was on the other side of the location when . . .").

Second, after the wrangler had rounded up his animals, there was an investigation. It was established that the explosion had been caused by a can of lighter fluid; it had been left too close to the fire it had helped to start, the one which two grips had made to boil coffee. Nobody, including Apple, was surprised when both young men fiercely denied having left the can anywhere near the fire. The horses had escaped from their corral by pressing against the rough-hewn, rope-hinged gate, which had collapsed.

Third and last, the caterer's van arrived from town. Its three women set about serving lunch. The hierarchy ate in their own wheeled quarters, others carried plates away, the majority gathered around the caterer's folding tables.

Apple's reason for staying near the van was to ask Bill about those two wanderers he had seen beyond the location. Apple wasn't pressing his own investigation of the crisis. He doubted (a) if there was anything to be learned, and knew (b) that he would bring suspicion on himself by too much nosiness. In any case he realised that the explosion could, indeed, have been due to accident and have nothing to do with either Clever Freddy or the laboratory people.

"I forget now," Bill said when Apple at last got the chance to ask his question. "You see so many people in a day, right? One of 'em coulda been Arthur Reed, though." He chewed, swallowed. "But how about you? Our hero."

Shrugging, Apple put on a modest expression. "Oh, it was nothing."

"Nothink?" the prop-man echoed loudly, gazing about with offended blinks to encourage an audience. "You call that nothink?" He went on to tell of the selfless act he had witnessed. He had many listeners.

Looking around slyly, Apple was disappointed to note

Velma Wilde's absence; then, with mixed emotions, to note the presence of someone whom he hadn't yet seen at close range— the wrangler.

His name, Apple had overheard, was Chuck Holt. American, he wore a shabby black outfit of tight gambler pants, lumber-jacket and stetson. The most prominent item under the hat brim was a Buffalo Bill goatee. The wrangler, who boarded at the town hotel, seemed to spend most of his workday in the background, with the horses.

Apple's feelings were mixed because of the professional and the private. Chuck Holt could be a prospect, and, while listening to the tale of bravery, he had a knowing smile.

Apple nearly blushed. That danger came closer when Cookie said, "Hey, let's hear it for the swashbuckler," and there was some banterish cheering. He was doing wonderfully, he told himself with sarcastic bite, at keeping a low profile.

The wrangler drifted away with a yawn. Apple followed one circumspect minute later, yawning also. He went around a caravan, from which came a snore. Another napper he stepped over before coming into an open patch. There was no sign of the man in baddy black.

Suspicion stronger, Apple was about to take a new direction when he saw an assistant director striding toward him. It was time to go to work.

From then until the workday's end, Monico performed for the camera. He did acceptably well. Through dozens of takes only twice did he fluff—once by beginning to scratch himself, once by snapping at a fly. Otherwise he responded dutifully to the signals and commands given him by Apple, who was out of the camera's reach.

Monico walked at an actor's heels in two of the shots, in a close-up licked a hand (it was coated with salmon paste), sat quietly through a long scene with sound, and chased after a pony (Apple running ahead). The director was satisfied.

During the evening wrap-up and departure, Apple's attention was given only to the night-watchman, who arrived on a bicycle. He turned out to be a stumpy, grumpy sixty-year-old with a vicious German shepherd. Apple wasn't interested. Neither was Monico.

Back at Blancairn, after being avoided on the bus by Johnny Fleming and ignored by Velma Wilde, Apple went straight up to his room. He had decided that there was little to be gained by appearing to be pursuing either of this pair.

Downstairs again following a shower and a change, Apple went in search of McKay, only to learn that the gardener had gone for the day. Gone where? Apple wondered.

In the dining-room, about to sit at a table with Cookie and others, Apple saw Wilson Croft through a window. The bearded security man was walking toward the parked vehicles. Apple went on watching.

Croft got into the small black Ford in which he had tailed the location motorcade. He drove to the road—Apple tensing —but then turned not toward the estate but town.

"Hey, Tim," Cookie laughed. "Are you going to stand there for ever?"

Town, Apple thought as he took a seat. That was an idea. Eat quickly and see what the big city had to offer, if only a close-up of Chuck Holt.

The King's Messenger was one of the flat-faced buildings siding the town square, where Apple parked. Its facade was of the same old grey stone as all the other buildings, so it gave Apple a shock when, followed by Monico, he entered a clash of bright colours and modern design.

What wasn't plastic was aluminium, and what wasn't new looked as though it was trying to be. With a long bar, crowded tables and loud, modern music, the lobby was as wrong in small-town Scotland as a cancan in church.

Apple was assured by seeing a score of familiar faces. Still on the threshold, he acknowledged waves with a lazy arm, but came alert on noting that one of the faces was coming this way. It belonged to the production manager.

They met. Apple said, "Good evening, Arthur."

"Evening," Arthur Reed said. "You have a problem?" He placed a spread hand over his bow-tie. "I was just leaving."

"No problems. Everything's fine. I wanted your advice on a matter. After all, you're the man who seems to know everything."

While Apple was telling himself that he was overdoing the flattery, Arthur Reed was nodding and lowering his hand. He asked, "On what can I advise you?"

Apple explained about his cousin with the mink farm. "He needs security people, you see, so I thought I'd ask you how you came to get hold of Wilson Croft."

"I didn't," Reed said in earnest, hand to chest like a confession of decency. "I imagine someone must have done the obvious thing—looked in the yellow pages." He smiled. "Right, if that's all . . ."

Apple said, "Well, there's the wrangler."

"Indeed there is. He made a super job today of rounding up his animals. We're all proud. Proud. But you mustn't let me delay you with my chatter. Good night." He went briskly past.

A slippery customer, Apple thought as he began to head for the bar counter. If that busy-busy manner was cover, it would be hard to beat for convenience. You could glib your way out of anything and still appear to be innocent.

After a couple of stops to exchange greetings, Apple reached the bar. He sat on a stool. His practicing of swivels stopped when one of the barmen came, leaned over and said quietly, "We don't want the likes of you in this establishment."

In time, before astonishment arrived, Apple recognised Rex. The fair-haired agent, wearing a white jacket, offered a smile that was void of humour. He said, "I kid in serious, Porter. What're you doing here?"

Apple gazed around. "Me?"

"You," Rex said, quietly testy. "This is my field of operations."

"I'm on a legit visit. I'm checking someone out."

"I'm the one here to check out anyone you sus. Who is it?"

The agent was perfectly correct, Apple realised with a prickle of discomfort. There was a certain protocol to be observed in these matters.

He said, "I'm joking. There's no suspect." As he obviously had no intentions of doing the right thing, passing on Chuck Holt, his discomfort continued.

"So what d'you want here?"

"To be honest, I came to see if I could get a look at Helen Parker. She won't be coming out to the location for a day or two yet."

"Help yourself," Rex said. "She's over there."

Apple swivelled, following the nod. Helen Parker, the film's supporting actress, was three tables away, sitting with two other women. Fan Apple, pleased, said lightly, "Think I'll go over and introduce myself."

The agent said, "You're out of your mind. She wouldn't squirt soda-water on you."

Apple's discomfort vanished and his pleasure thrived. "Oh, I don't know," he said, absorbing the actress.

Helen Parker was petite. She wore a simple dress of folksy cotton. Her tanned, cosmetics-free face was cute more than pretty. It was complemented immaculately by the hair cut in urchin style.

Apple glanced aside. "Sherry on the rocks, please."

Rex asked in a drawl, "Do you think you should?"

It was because of that, Apple supposed, that he got up and went toward where the three women sat. He was still vaguely hoping that he wouldn't go through with it when he stopped at the table.

The trio, two of whom Apple recognised as being with wardrobe, looked up at him quizzically. After nodding around he bent toward the actress, saying, "May I introduce myself, Miss Parker? Tim Gordon. I'm also on this movie."

With mild interest: "Are you in the production department, Mr. Gordon?"

"No, I handle the dog," Apple said, gesturing behind him but then seeing that Monico was still near the bar, being fed peanuts by a customer.

With no interest whatever, Helen Parker asked, "The dog?"

"Yes. There's a dog in *My Candle Burns.*"

"I've only read my own part of the script, I'm afraid," the supporting actress said. "Nice meeting you." She looked down.

Apple: "His name's Monico."

"Fine."

"And he's a great actor."

Sighing, Helen Parker looked up again. She put a hand to the back of her neck and said levelly, "The only good animal actor in motion-picture history was a lady called Lassie."

Delighted at being able to impress with one of the tidbits of movie lore which he had recently learned at Damian House, Apple said, "Lassie, you know, was always played by a male dog."

Straightening, Helen Parker leaned toward her friends. "As I was saying . . ."

Apple said he thought he would be running along now. The women ignored him. Smiling loosely, his imagination semi-picturing a bed of hot coals just in case, Apple moved away. He didn't glance back at the bar to see if Rex was watching.

Getting the cold shoulder was his own fault, Apple mused. He ought to have remembered, along with that tidbit, how stars hated to be outdone in knowledge of filmdom lore, especially by people who were low down in the pecking order. But it didn't matter. He had casually bandied words with the famous Helen Parker.

Uncalled for, the hovering Indian market-place faded, and Apple concentrated on trying to look nonchalant as he scanned around for sight of the wrangler. He was absent.

Apple circled slowly, as others were doing. It was a lively scene and he was loathe to leave. But he no longer had a reason for staying, as far as Rex was concerned. And if he did see Chuck Holt, he couldn't very well approach him. It would, in fact, be wrong to. Fair was fair.

Apple's conscience made him decide to go. What then made him decide to hurry, pushed him into striding, was the thought that his conscience might make him next tell Rex how strongly he suspected the wrangler.

It was dark outside. The square was as good as deserted, except for parked cars. Apple went to his Austin, put Monico in the back, got inside, fastened his safety belt, started the motor and drove off.

While talking to Monico about the situation, Apple reached back and stroked the wire mesh that separated cab from body. This was to show Monico that, although the mesh went with TIM'S KENNELS, Apple didn't approve of the segregating device. He stroked with the back of his hand because once, on the journey from London, with his hand reversed, he had caught his fingers in the mesh and had needed to come to a fast halt.

They left the small town and its suburbs behind within minutes. Another seven or eight minutes on the quiet secondary road would bring them to the guest-house.

With no traffic in sight—though a car with bright lights was behind—Apple picked up speeed as, doing all the talking, he argued with his dog about which field of operations Chuck Holt fell into—where he lodged or where he worked. Monico, lying on a rug, yawned squeakily.

"It's a matter of his career life as opposed to his private," Apple said. "That's what it amounts to. It's perfectly kosher for me to . . ."

Apple let it go because the headlights behind were dazzling him via his rear-view mirror. He reckoned that the car must be coming along at much more than his own speed, which was sixty.

The road ahead was clear and straight, lit to its limits by the Austin's own lights. After twisting his mirror up, Apple steered closer into the side of the road, at the same time putting an arm through the window space and waving a pass-by.

The car stayed behind. Apple waved again, sweeping his arm forcefully. The car stayed put.

With a mental shrug, Apple reminded himself that, after all, the driver had neither flashed his lights nor blown his horn to indicate that he wanted to pass.

Apple adjusted his mirror, suddenly thinking Mission. But he at once dismissed the possibility that he was being tailed. No one would come this close.

In the rear-view, even with his eyes slitted, Apple could see only glare. He turned his head for a quick look back. The headlights were too strong for him to make out anything other than the fact that the car was large.

Apple had just turned front again when the hit came.

It jerked the van forward, snapped Apple's upper body into a whiplash, threw Monico against the wire mesh.

"Christ," Apple gasped, shocked. "The idiot." He told Monico, who was getting up, "Don't worry."

Giving a thankful pat to his safety-belt, Apple thought that if the driver wasn't a maniac or a drunk, he could only be an enemy. Whatever, there was no sense in trying to find out which, not right at this moment.

Apple slammed his foot flat on the accelerator. The little van responded well. It spurted forward. The speedometer needle climbed to seventy.

The chase car fell back. But only briefly. Its lights grew more powerful as they came quickly on. And on.

Apple braced for the hit. He told himself he wasn't afraid. He told it also to Monico, who was standing in a lean against the mesh.

The big car struck hard, with a loud clang. The van jerked off-course as it was kicked forward.

Apple swore. But, having been prepared, there was only mild whiplash and he was able to correct the van's aim. He had more concern for his dog, who had crashed to rear door and back to mesh. Monico, unheld, could seriously injure himself.

His foot still firmly to the floor, the Austin still gathering speed, Apple ordered, "Down." Immediately, Monico lay on his rug.

Between fast glances in the mirror, Apple scanned the way ahead. He needed to get off this road, to where he would have the seconds needed to safely stop. He would then get out, and the situation would be different.

There were no breaks, however, in the hedges that grew a yard high on either side of the narrow road; the road which now went into a right-hand curve. Apple took it at nearly eighty miles an hour.

From behind came a squeal of brakes coupled with a fading of the glare. It told Apple that the advantage had been his in being able to see the curve's severity. It also told him that the car was probably a Jaguar.

There was another bend, going left. Apple took it with again no reduction of speed. His fear was constant—for both Monico and himself.

After the bend came a humpbacked bridge. The van left the ground briefly as it shot off the far side, landing with a thump and a shimmy.

Seconds later came another thud—from behind. The chase car was catching up.

Again the road was straight. Right behind the hedges were thick-trunked trees. Being knocked into one of those would be no joke, Apple thought as he sped along smack in the middle of the road.

Ahead, lights flashed into view. A vehicle was coming. Apple hoped that it would be of use. But the big car was closing in fast for another strike. Apple began to brace himself.

The vehicle ahead was a bus. That became clear when now its driver obeyed rules and dipped his headlights. Apple did the same. The big car's lights, which looked to have stopped gaining, stayed up, even after repeat flashes from the bus.

Apple didn't like that ruthlessness. And his fear gathered strength as he realised that the mystery driver, taking this opportunity, could be holding back in order to make his hit just when the van was drawing close to the bus.

The lights ahead were still flashing at angry speed. Apple would have flashed back in a near-pointless attempt at a warning if he had been less occupied with driving the van.

He drew it into his own side of the road: the bus was almost here. So was the hit-and-chase car.

Apple stared ahead. He gripped the wheel rigidly. He steeled his body. He was acutely aware that the glare from behind was directly at the van's rear. He wondered what would become of Ethel.

The small van was trembling, hitting its limits at eighty-five miles an hour. The bus was only a dozen feet away. Its driver, sitting high, could be seen clearly in the lights. He was scowling.

Simultaneously, Apple heard a clang and felt a lurch. The hit had knocked his Austin only a foot off-track. At eighty-five miles per hour the big car lacked the spurt of lower speeds.

Apple was able to correct in time, before the noses of van and bus careened past each other. But he shuddered at the sick closeness of it.

There was another lurch, slighter than the last. Then another with even less force. The accompanying clangs had been feeble.

Apple realised that the two vehicles were now in continuing touch; next, as the speedometer needle started going beyond eighty-five, that the van was being pushed.

Holding on grimly, his mouth open and dry, Apple tried to think of a countering technique. No situations like this had been dealt with in Training Five.

Not until the needle was dithering against ninety did it occur to Apple to resist the push. He saw that if he didn't, he was in danger of being rammed into the first immovable object that they came to, with the big car avoiding the crash by braking at the last moment.

Fortunately, there was nothing at present on either side but the low hedges, though anything could be hidden in the darkness beyond.

Apple put his foot hard on the brake. The needle drooped at once. It continued to do so, soon reaching eighty. Apple brought it down to seventy by pulling on the parking-brake, then arrived near sixty by changing to a lower gear.

The transmission was screaming, Monico was whining and brake linings were burning, but Apple stuck fiercely to his strategy. Not for a second did he take his eyes off the road, across which he was tacking as the victim of rear force.

The needle was still sinking, and Apple was curling on a

tentative smile of victory, when his lights lit up a sign. It warned to reduce speed to thirty miles per hour for the dangerous bend ahead.

Apple put the foot-brake pedal down as far as it would go. The Austin went into an immediate swerve. His heart leaping, Apple ended that by letting the pedal up—and up too far. The van was swept forward with new impetus.

The smell of burning had made Apple's eyes start to sting. He was blinking as the van went into the left-hand bend at over sixty miles an hour.

It was too fast.

The van began easing over toward the bend's outer curve. Apple, his heart holding on, saw that there was no way he could avoid hitting the hedge. It was inevitable.

Therefore he decided that he would hit it under his own control, and direct instead of side-swipe.

He turned the steering-wheel to his right. The Austin shot off as if in relief in the direction it had been fighting—straight for the hedge. There was a change in velocity as the two vehicles lost contact.

The van smashed into the hedge nose-first with a noise like a bar-room brawl. Up flew a barrage of twigs and leaves and undergrowth.

That was left behind in an instant. The windshield cleared. Ahead, luckily, lay an open field. Unluckily, it sloped downward towards a brook.

Knowing that he had to avoid reaching that point, Apple braked. As expected, the small van went into a spin.

It swung completely around time after time, with Monico rumpling about in the back and Apple holding on tightly as he stared at the whirling countryside.

In the sweep of headlights the brook came and went, came and went. It grew closer with every turn.

A crash sounded from below. A rock, Apple guessed.

Straight away the Austin began to tilt. Still spinning, it rose up on to two wheels. Next, it crashed right over. It went on twirling crunchingly on its side.

The twirls slowed. The van came to a gentle, quiet halt like a subsiding dervish.

After looking behind to make sure that Monico was merely outraged, not hurt, Apple, who was on the down side, relaxed in order to collect himself. For the feeling of security, he put a hand on the grass that filled the window space.

There came the faint sound of voices.

The next moment a blurred face appeared. It was beyond the passenger-side window, directly above Apple. Reflections made identification impossible. Reaching up, Apple wound the window down. The face was one he knew. It belonged to the bland prop-man, Johnny Fleming.

He asked breathlessly, "You all right?"

"Not a scratch," Apple said. "But what on earth are you doing here?"

"I was tailing you daredevils on a motor bike," Johnny Fleming said. "I'm your back-up."

THREE

Next morning shooting went so well, and Monico performed so perfectly, that at lunch someone remarked, "Nothing like a jinx to help things along." Everyone nearby laughed, apart from Cookie, who pulled a sour face.

Soon she moved over to sit beside Apple. Following their agreement on the excellence of the Scotch broth, among other idle chat, Cookie said, "He's a peculiar guy, that prop-man you were talking to earlier."

"I was talking to?" Apple said warily.

"Yeah. On the bus."

"Oh, that one. I thought he was a grip. Joe or Jack or something like that."

Cookie resettled her purple wig. "He's called Johnny Fleming and he's in props, and I think he's peculiar."

Apple said softeningly, "All movie people're a bit strange."

But Cookie wasn't going to be put off with a generalisation. Giving a shoulder-shuffle she said, "For one thing, he keeps out of everybody's way. And there's what he said to me this morning, about the clapper-board, which was real odd."

"What did he say about the slate?" Apple asked, neatly getting in another cant term.

"Well, when we're not recording here, the board has the usual MOS initials on it, and surely a man like Fleming would know what it stood for, wouldn't you think?"

Apple filled his mouth with food while racing through the index files in his memory. He recalled that MOS, formed originally in jest from the accents of the many Europeans who were working in Hollywood, stood for Mit Out Sound.

After making sure that Cookie knew that he knew, Apple said, "That Fleming character's putting you on. He knows this business backwards."

"Well . . . maybe."

"But listen. Let me tell you about my accident."

Cookie became the latest of several recipients of the story, including wrangler Chuck Holt and Arthur Reed, neither of whom had responded as if he knew that Apple was lying when he told about his van hitting a slippery patch of road and skidding through a hedge.

Cookie's response was a suspicious "You think something oily had been put on the road?"

"Dew, kid," Apple said, noting with pride the way his speech was taking on a slickness to match his role. "You can forget sabotage."

He went on to tell the truth, how several motorists had come, had helped right the van (battered but operational), and how he had telephoned to the police a false report of the incident.

Cookie hid her boredom badly, but when the story was over she didn't go back to the subject of the pseudo prop-man, to Apple's relief. There was enough to do in keeping his own cover intact, he thought, without having to protect that of a colleague.

Last night Johnny Fleming hadn't had time to say much before the motorists had started to arrive, at which point he had slipped away without being seen. This morning, on the bus, he had frowned as Apple took the seat beside him.

"Old Angus wouldn't like this."

"Since you're the one who's watching me, he'd only know if you told him."

"Could be other finks of his around. But I'm not mentioning

anything, and don't you even say you know I'm alive. Please ignore me from now on."

"That goes both ways. I like a clear field, so don't trail me around. That's the message I bring you."

"I'll do what orders tell me to do."

"What do they tell you about the caper?"

"Only that some spynik is nosing out a lab."

"He's free lance, not a Soviet," Apple said, and left it there. He was greedy with his info. He didn't want Fleming trying to get in on the act, which back-up men sometimes did, and which Apple knew he himself would do if he were in Fleming's place.

"See you around," Apple had said in conclusion, rising. "From a distance."

Now, not listening as Cookie talked shop, Apple told himself that maybe he shouldn't have been so cool with his back-up. He might need his help sometime. Clever Freddy had definitely meant terminal business last night in what was undoubtedly a stolen car. But the film location, at least, had to be a sanctuary. If anyone got killed here, the place would be aswarm with policemen, which would suit nobody.

An assistant director began to go around clapping his hands and calling, "Out of the trough, gang." The lunch break had come to an end.

For the following hour, Monico not being needed yet, Apple had the chance to snoop. His mind was evasive, however; it kept reminding him of what he had learned from the call-sheet which he had found under his door last night: the fabulous Miranda Wheldon would be filming this afternoon.

When the movie goddess arrived, forty-five minutes late, Apple was delighted to see that her limousine was a pink Cadillac of Ethel's generation. Its owner was even more flamboyant.

One of the few survivors of an endangered species, la

Wheldon was attended by a maid, a hairdresser, a secretary, a stand-in, two middle-aged admirers, a press agent and a pair of huge bodyguards. Some of these courtiers came in a second car, a Rolls-Royce that looked weeks old.

Miranda Wheldon was tall and voluptuous ("big and fat," Cookie whispered). She had beautiful teeth ("caps") and long blond hair ("bleach"). Her breasts were astonishing ("silicone"). She had a beautiful, smooth-skinned face and she appeared to be in her late twenties ("plastic surgery; forty-six at least").

"Who cares about the stage-dressing?" Apple said as they watched the actress being escorted to her lavish trailer. "She is a knock-out, and she still has her symbolism."

"Hey, you sound like a red-hot movie fan."

Alerting, Apple laughed. "Cookie," he said, "you just have to learn when someone's putting you on." Moving off, he told himself: Watch it, faceless one.

The rest of the day's shooting went well. Only three takes were needed to get Monico's seven-second shot with Miranda Wheldon, after he and Apple had been introduced to her. She gave the dog more attention than his owner, whom she dismissed politely with "Are you always so tall, darling?"

In the bus, ignoring a twinge of guilt at not having been thinking Mission strongly enough, Apple decided that Monico looked a bit on the heavy side. It would be better if he got less meat tonight.

Off the bus first, Apple went straight around to the back of Blancairn. There he was almost run into by a pedal bicycle. Its frame was the racing type and its rider was a man of about thirty-five. He looked sturdily built under his green coveralls. Short hair topped a face that was plain verging on ugly.

"Well?" he asked smilingly of Apple, who remained standing in the place where he had come to a jerked stop. "Can I pass?" His accent was a guttural Glaswegian.

"Ah," Apple said slowly. He was realising that he hadn't the slightest idea of how to talk to the gardener. There was no point of reference.

Again the man asked, "Well?"

Apple said, "You must be Mr. McKay."

"That's right. I must."

"Well, Mr. McKay, I was told that you knew something about winter roses."

"Och, not so much," the gardener said cheerfully, following which he went on to cover the subject like a professor of horticulture.

He went on so long that Apple began to feel that if this was Clever Freddy, then Clever Freddy was a genius. The accent was perfect, the easy manner so good it was likeable, the information rich with the tone of veracity. Apple also began to feel bored.

It wasn't until he had got away from McKay, who seemed prepared to talk all night, that Apple reminded himself that the free lance spy, besides being an excellent mimic and actor, could also be the type of person who had a store of odd data in his memory. Some people were funny that way.

The new gardener, Apple decided, had to be added to the list of chief suspects, along with Chuck Holt, Arthur Reed and Wilson Croft.

Reversewise, Apple knew that he himself was on Clever Freddy's list of suspected counterspies, if not suspect number one, so he had to be on his toes when away from the location sanctuary. Nor would it hurt if he worked harder at playing innocent dog-handler.

For the rest of the evening, after he had got Monico his dinner plus an extra ration of meat, Apple kept to himself. He spoke to no one until he had gone to his room. There, before retiring, he called the hotel in town. He asked for the barman by description, not possessing a cover name, and told Rex that

Chuck Holt the wrangler seemed a hot possibility. He didn't mind receiving a snapped "You think I'm blind?" He knew he would sleep tonight.

Even Cookie had to agree that the next morning's shooting hit the jinxless norm. Tempers were lost, Helen Parker spoiled a series of takes by laughing, the actor-director snarled at his assistants, a cloud came over at the wrong moment, and film nevertheless went into the can.

Monico's contribution was sniffing under the skirt of the maid he was following in his one scene of the day. That maid was Velma Wilde. She gave Apple a look like an executioner, Monico a kick on the sly.

Free, Apple strolled to the location's edge, past the last cable, box and generator. Behind him there was no one to be seen because of intervening equipment. Ahead lay countryside, with fir trees and small buttes of rock rising from the heavily undulating ground, which had scatterings of heather.

Apple went on strolling. With Monico bounding on in front, he headed for the nearest bunch of firs. He was midway there when a man came into view from between the trunks. It was Wilson Croft in his quasi-uniform.

They met and stopped. Apple said, "I'm always seeing you lurking in trees."

"Very funny," the bearded man said. "You film people never take off the clown make-up."

"I'm really just a dog-handler, not film folk, and I'm giving my dog a run. How far can I go?"

Wilson Croft shook his head, but in friendly fashion. "I'm sorry. I think this is far enough. We don't want to get the estate's owners angry with us, do we?"

Together they moved back toward the location. Croft said, "I hear you had an accident the other night."

"I certainly did."

"You skidded on a slick patch, eh?"

It wasn't until Apple had given an affirmative that he saw this as the wrong answer—possibly. If the security man was Clever Freddy, hence the big car's driver, he would know the truth. Which meant that a lie would establish for him Tim Gordon as a counterspy.

Apple brought Wilson Croft to a halt. "Listen," he said after looking over his shoulder. "I made that story up."

Croft stroked his beard. "Oh?"

"I can tell you the truth because, in a way, you're somewhere between a citizen and a policeman. Maybe you can give me some advice. But keep this to yourself, if you don't mind."

"You sound very mysterious."

Apple said, "It's just that I wouldn't want a certain person to get into trouble. See, this person was driving drunk the other night." He went on to give a fairly accurate description of the chase and bumping.

Wilson Croft asked, "You saw the driver's face?"

"Not clearly, but I'm sure I know who it is."

"You could always check cars. You know, look for marks on the front bumper."

Apple shook his head. "Listen. I don't care. No real harm's been done, and I have my job to think of. But what d'you think? Should I tell the police the real story, without saying that I know who it was?"

Still looking up at him and stroking his beard, the security man ambled through a mild sermon on the falsification of statements. Apple said he would think about it.

Walking on to the location alone a minute later, he told himself how shrewd and pro-like he had been in approaching Croft with the truth.

On the set, the village street, there was one last shot before lunch. It was a solo for the supporting actress, Helen Parker.

Apple, watching, caught her eye between takes. He sent a wave. She nodded at him as you would at a number on a door.

Filming over, Helen Parker and honoured others went off to lunch in the director's caravan—movie location equivalent of the captain's table. Apple joined a group around the caterer's layout.

Someone was handing out paper cups full of Scotch broth. Apple got one. After finishing that he queued up for shepherd's pie. Next came peaches in cream, cheese and biscuits, coffee or milk.

Replete, Apple found a sunny patch of grass between two trucks. He lay down with Monico beside him, closed his eyes and relaxed.

He continued relaxing as a small white cloud came down from the sky, picked him up softly and carried him away.

It was a delicious dream. Apple was sorry when it ended, when the cloud put him back down after a heavenly ride. With reluctance he came awake and opened his eyes.

For a minute or two he lay still. He was comfortable in mind as well as body. Then came a niggly thought: Was it not a little curious that he'd had a post-lunch catnap, which was almost unknown to him?

He looked at his watch. With a surprise that made him sit up, he saw that he had been asleep for nearly an hour.

Being no longer comfortable in mind, Apple realised that he wasn't perfectly so in body, either. There was a faint tingle at the nape of his neck, also a hint of acidity in his mouth. He had no need to add the evidence of the delightful dream in order to deduce, from what he had learned in Training Seven, that he had been drugged.

Bloody neat, Apple thought in admiration. Clever Freddy slips a soporific into my food and has the best part of an hour to do a scouring tour of the countryside.

Apple's next thought was: But what if he hadn't yet come back here?

He jumped up quickly. Hurrying, he went to the location's rim. Beyond there, he saw no one. He walked on around the crescent, still looking.

On the subject of drug introduction, Apple mused that it could have been done at any time during the lunch break, which he had spent in close proximity with others, though with none of the suspects. Clever Freddy would have had few problems in reaching over a shoulder or under an arm, or even in tossing a pellet from nearby.

However, Apple was backing the Scotch broth as the carrying agent, for its consistency and mixed flavours were ideal for hiding an alien additive. The cup, furthermore, had been as good as put into his hand. But he couldn't recall by whom, and it certainly wouldn't have been by Freddy himself.

Having seen nothing suspicious on reaching the end of the crescent, Apple turned.

The scream came as he started back.

He changed course and ran into the equipment.

Getting clear of a bus, Apple was able to both see and feel what had caused that first scream, and what was causing more of the similar. It was like walking outdoors into a gale.

Stopping as the blast tore at his face, hair and clothing, Apple fell into a protective crouch and ordered Monico to lie down. Through near-closed eyes he stared around at the scene of panic.

The wind machine was switched on.

This monster version of a domestic fan, man-height, was hurtling air across a wedge of the location. Dust flew everywhere, papers were sent soaring aloft, canvas chairs bowled along like tumbleweed.

Cast yelled for help; crew bellowed orders. Most people were either lying flat or moving in a crouch. Some were fighting their way into the gale's maw. Squealing as she went, a wardrobe girl was being forced along at an all-out run. Trailer doors banged and the unsolid wobbled or leaned.

Apple, fascinated by the weird scene, went on staring. He saw lightweight pieces of equipment crash over; saw a black stetson hat and two shirts go flying by; saw, dimly through the dust, men circling to the wind machine's rear.

Turning away, Apple ran to help.

Within seconds he was farther along the crescent and out of the blast. Next he was arriving behind the giant fan—and in turbulence again, from the suction.

Reading between the shouts of the men at the machine's control box, Apple gathered that the switch was jammed—on HIGH. One grip was prising at it with a screwdriver, his shirt and hair dancing madly.

He was still doing this when the fan's whine lost its keening pitch. It continued to descend the scale while the large blades began to slow and the air turbulence lessened. The grip stood back. He and Apple and the others turned as the hatless wrangler came into view, a cable end in his hand.

Chuck Holt said coolly, "I disconnected from the power."

The inquest lasted throughout the rest of the day and into the evening. What had started in like a lion, emotionally, went out like a lamb. Easement came from the fact that shooting got under way within half an hour, nothing was even slightly dented and nobody was hurt beyond dust in the eyes.

The only person who could claim to have suffered was the script supervisor. That half-hour she spent blinking worriedly through her heart-shaped glasses while collecting and sorting her papers.

It was established that the wind machine must have been damaged in transit (it hadn't been tried here), and that the cable's two ends must have been seen and connected by someone (who was trying to be useful and was not expected to own up to his mistake).

By the time dinner at the guest-house was over, the incident had become a joke called Hurricane Velma, due to the bit player having put on the most hammy performance of maiden-in-distress. Even Cookie laughed, though she went on looking satisfied.

Apple's satisfaction came from knowing that he who can find and tear asunder could also have found and made as one. Also from knowing that two disruptive incidents in a row was one too many, so if Hurricane Velma was an accident, the Cavalry Stampede had been sabotage, or vice versa.

But Clever Freddy, if the culprit, wasn't having much luck in delaying shooting for long in order to lengthen the stay here, and if the laboratory people were the villains, they were being equally unsuccessful in getting the film company to pack up and leave.

At nine o'clock, having got nowhere with his casual questions on the subject of who had handed out the broth, Apple decided to go out on the prowl. At the door he halted on seeing that rain was falling heavily.

Monico turned away at once. His owner followed. They went up to their room for the night.

Apple told himself he was keeping a low profile, not responding to the fact that he was no longer on the location santuary. Until he fell asleep, he read a spy novel.

When the desk rang next morning, it wasn't a wake-up call but the news that, because of rain, shooting had been cancelled. Apple turned over and went to sleep again.

Later he joined others in the lounge for mid-morning coffee and rolls. It was still raining. Apple wasn't worried that Clever Freddy might be out and about on the snoop; his absence in such foul weather would, obviously, be remarked on by a counterspy.

Apple socialised, his sole Mission thought in connection with Johnny Fleming. While pleased that his back-up was keeping well in the background, he thought that he was trying far too hard for general dimming of presence. Apple decided to have a word with Fleming on that score. This gave him a warm, spymaster feeling. He made the decision again.

Before lunch, a late affair, Apple had the chance to talk to the severe proprietress of Blancairn. He learned nothing that would help his mink-farmer cousin find a good gardener.

Lunch over, there was more of the same in the lounge, with everyone growing lethargic. Monico kept yawning. When Apple also became bored, he strolled away and left the house quietly by a rear door. He ran through the rain to his battered, mud-streaked Austin van.

With Monico in the passenger seat, Apple drove out to the estate, stopping near the gate, which was padlocked. He stayed there for an hour, feeling diligent.

Once, braving the downpour, he got out to look over the wall at the pigs wallowing in their pen. It was the smell more than the rain that drove him back inside.

Later on, an ancient van rolled up. Apple had his eyes narrowed until an old, bent man, a grey beard showing under the sack he wore over his head, opened the van doors and began to unload pigswill. Apple left.

Back at the guest-house, Apple at once noted that the lethargy had gone. Limping over to him with a grin, Cookie said, "Hey, that's the way she is—impulsive. But there's more to it than that, of course."

"I don't doubt it for a moment."

"She's also looking for assurance that she's still a candle for us moths."

"Quite."

"And candle is right. Miranda's fading. There's no other movie in view, and they say she puts on a pound of weight a day. It can't be long now. So she's playing movie queen right up to the hilt."

"I'm sure she is," Apple said. "But I don't know what you're talking about."

"Sorry, thought you'd heard," Cookie said. "It's Miranda Wheldon. She's invited everyone in the movie mob to her mansion tonight. A party."

It wasn't until afterwards, in the van, that it occurred to Apple that the mansion was no more a sanctuary than the guest-house was.

Although the residence was floodlit as lavishly as a theatre on premier night, the design itself was straightforward nineteenth-century Scottish Laird: plain and stern. Inside, the lavish came in the form of Christmas decorations, with tinsel and paper-chains strung around the baronial hall.

There was already a goodly crowd when Apple arrived with the guest-house contingent. Of the two long side-tables, one for food and one for drink, the latter had the most custom. In one corner, a two-piece accordion band was being defeated by a pop tune.

Hostess and courtiers were sitting by the foot of the broad staircase. After his obligatory visit there, to salaam Miranda Wheldon, who said, there he was, at it again, Apple got a sherry on the rocks and found a place to stand with his back to a wall. He was glad he had left Monico at home.

Everything was clear to Apple's high view. He picked out Chuck Holt, still in wrangler black, plus stetson; Wilson Croft in a lounge suit that was almost as dark as his beard; Velma Wilde just about wearing a low, short dress; Cookie looking smart in a trouser-suit and a plaid wig.

Apple also worked at picking out the strangers who would make good Clever Freddy material. He was relieved to see only two who could be possibles.

Half an hour passed.

Apple began to relax, as well as to enjoy being boldly dressed: over his roll-neck jersey he wore the yellow blazer that was a souvenir of the Curious Affair at Harp Hall. He left his post and got a leg of chicken.

Late guests arrived, tailed after a pause by the movie's number-two actress Helen Parker. Her entrance was marred on account of the shrieks of laughter which arose suddenly, and without apparent cause, from the region of the stairs.

Dancing began. Apple, wiping his hands after a second leg of chicken, moved into the circle of sideliners. He wondered if he had the nerve to ask one of the three women he most wanted to hold in his arms if she would care to dance, so he could tell about it.

Into Apple's path came a matron who topped out at five feet ten inches. "Come along, Tim," she said, jolly-commanding. "It's not often I get the chance to hop with someone I'm not looking down on."

Apple's understanding ran dry with the sixth dance. With a reference to his fallen arches, he excused himself from the woman, who was with the make-up department, and went towards where he had last seen Johnny Fleming.

Instead of his back-up, Apple found Arthur Reed in the squeeze by the makeshift bar. The production man was immaculate in a riding outfit, which he explained with, "I'd just got back from hacking when I heard about the party." It sounded as if he was sick to death of saying the same thing. He hurried on with "That accident of yours."

"It was nothing."

Arthur Reed edged closer, lowered his voice. "A little bird told me that you were quite . . . well . . . drunk."

"A little bird? Sounds more like a little rodent."

"Whomever," Reed said. "It's the fact that matters." He

began a polite lecture on the inadvisability of breaking the law and thus giving the film unit a bad image.

Neat follow-up, Apple thought. Clever Freddy (if other than the production manager himself) fails at the car bumping but uses it to try to get the dog-handler in trouble, and perhaps even fired. Monico had been in too many scenes, however, for him to be changed now. The job was safe.

Holding up a hand to stop the lecture, Apple said, "I won't go into details about my so-called accident. It's a closed chapter. Suffice it to say that I was not drunk in the least."

Following a nod, Arthur Reed went straight back to his lecture. Apple caused the voice to fade simply by straightening up out of his listener's stoop. He then saw Johnny Fleming and, with the same kind of nod that the production man had just given, moved away.

The crowd denser now, as well as noisier, it was several minutes before Apple caught up to Fleming, who was circling the room by the wall.

Apple took his arm with, "Come to the party and smile."

"I am. My smile's on the inside."

"Seriously. You're being too off-putting with the others. It's being noticed."

Coldly, Johnny Fleming asked, "Is that all, sir?"

Feeling uncomfortable, Apple said, "Don't be dense. I'm only trying to help."

"Then I suggest you help us both by not dogging my footsteps. I'm supposed to dog yours."

"Don't you dare."

"So long, boss-man," Fleming said, edging away.

From watching him leave, Apple turned at the sound of a hiss. Through an ajar door, standing back in dimness, was a man in uniform. From its beige and green colouring Apple knew the wearer to belong to a nationally known security firm. The last thing he recognised was the face.

With a glance around, Apple went across to the doorway. He asked, "You hissed?"

Stan, the dark-haired operative, accused, "You're playing counterspy on my territory."

"Wrong. That was my back-up."

The agent blinked. "*I* don't have a back-up."

Instead of saying "You probably do have one around here somewhere," Apple murmured a blasé "Oh?"

Looking as if he wished he hadn't spoken, Stan said, "You've also been nosing around at the hotel in town, I hear. That's fine with me. Stay there. Myself, I don't care for stampedes and car accidents and suchlike. Some of us want to keep our profiles real low."

Apple sought a retort. "I'm glad we ran into each other," he said after a moment. "I'd forgotten all about you." It was better than nothing, he thought, but he then had to admit that, as it was true, it didn't really count. He just wasn't much good at this sort of thing.

"Lovely," Stan said. "Keep forgetting." He closed the door. It missed meeting Apple's nose by an inch.

Moving off, heading back towards the bar, Apple left Mission and returned to wondering about the dancing partners he would like to have.

He was still wondering, having finished his sherry on the rocks, when all the lights went out.

In the instant, Apple dropped to his hands and knees. He hit the floor even before the crowd had responded with the standard: a crow which had the tone of appreciation but was actually there to hide the worry.

The sound started to turn sentimental and relieved, for the pseudo-darkness was lightening—from the candelabra on both side-tables.

Quickly, before he was seen, or sat on, Apple jumped up. He laughed just in case. It was all right. The hot prickle on his chest already cooling, he began to move at an easy pace through the mellow-lit crowd.

At the side Apple stood with his shoulders to the wall. He intended staying like that, though not in the same spot, which would have looked suspicious.

After five minutes he moved. The next time he moved was because he saw the tall make-up woman approaching with dance in her eyes. The third time it was when a hiss sounded from a nearby doorway.

Apple stepped from the wall to get a better sighting. Through the ajar door it was dark. Then came a flash of light. It was from a flashlight that was being held in someone's hand. Apple went to the doorway.

The someone, several yards back along a passage, was only a vague shape above the disc of brightness thrown on the floor by the flashlight.

Apple pushed on the door and slipped inside.

The flashlight moved farther back, making as it did a jerk like a come-on gesture. Its direct beam was going around a corner as Apple closed the door behind him. He went forward. The party noise faded.

Not telling himself that this could be Velma, whose filmdom rank consciousness wouldn't let her get friendly with a lowly animal-handler, unless it was in secret, Apple went to the passage corner. He was in darkness except for the backwash from the flashlight.

This was causing stripes of shadow, Apple saw when he had rounded the turning. The stripes were from banister rails. The person was going up a flight of stairs.

"Hello?" Apple said tentatively.

The response was a warning-like hiss accompanied by another jerk of the flashlight. Apple, lolling slightly at his crassness, while at the same time wondering if he was being obtuse, stepped on to the stairs and began to go up quietly.

The flashlight beam was directed back down, which made it easy for Apple to see his way. But it also meant that the bearer was an even vaguer shape than before.

The beam flicked away. Apple continued up by touch. He reached the level, which had a glow of bluish light that was unconnected with the flashlight. It came through a window and was caused by the floodlighting.

The person had passed through a doorway. Impatient to know, Apple went there in fast strides. He slowed again to caution, however, as he went inside.

It seemed to be a dressing-room. Dimly seen were racks of clothes and a vanity table. Windowless, light came only from ahead, where the flashlight, unmoving, played its beam on the floor. The stillness seemed to indicate that the journey was now completed.

"Hello there," Apple said softly. When there was no answer, he started to cross the room. At the midway point he heard a thud from behind. He whirled. It was the door. It had closed. Frowning, not happy with the situation, Apple turned and went on.

He became less happy when, even before reaching it, he saw that the flashlight now had no bearer; it was hooked onto the pocket of a garment.

The bearer, Apple thought in self-disgust, had obviously just left, after successfully bringing off one of the oldest tricks in the game. But to what purpose?

Apple mulled it over as he unhooked the flashlight and went back to the door to check that it was, as expected, locked (never take anything for granted, they taught in Training Three). Locked it was, with a modern unpickable lock.

All that occurred to Apple was an irony, one which he knew ought to have come to him before. What if laboratory security had been checking covers, had found Tim Gordon's feeble, or phony, had therefore concluded that he was Clever Freddy, and were endeavouring to frighten him off?

Although this was likeable, the last part wasn't likely, Apple mused. Despite Angus Watkin's sub-poor opinion of the laboratory people, they would be sure to realise that the ploy could only serve to convince Clever Freddy of their secret lab's existence.

What Apple found likeable about it was the idea of being caught between two fires. That was the stuff of classic espionage.

And now he was caught in a locked room, alone, Apple thought. But was he alone after all? Wasn't that someone over there hissing?

Apple listened acutely. There was a hiss, yes, but it was continuous, without a break for breath. So it couldn't be coming from a person.

The answer was supplied by another sense—smell. It treated Apple to that faint, rotting-cabbage fragrance of domestic gas. He felt chilled.

Turning quickly back to the door, he battered it hard with both fists. He also shouted, "Hey, open up!" He didn't persist with either hits or shouts. With all the racket going on below, it was improbable that he would be heard, at least by anyone who would be willing to help.

The source of the gas. That, Apple told himself urgently, was what he had to find. And with fair speed. Before the fumes got into his head. Made him muzzy. Confused.

Grateful for the flashlight, Apple made a fast tour of the room, looking and listening. The hiss was loudest behind a rack of clothes. He moved it.

There was a hearth. It had an old-fashioned gas fire. The pipe had been ripped up from its connection somewhere underneath the floor. Gas was seeping upward in a dozen places through the tiles. It would be impossible to block it off. The only hope was to break through to the connection.

While darting around the room in search of a tool or a heavy object, Apple acknowledged that the trick had been neatly done. Clever Freddy switches off the gas at the main, breaks the pipe, lures his victim to the trap, locks him in and puts the switch on again.

Apple came across nothing that he could make use of as a tool. He went on searching, ripping open drawers and throwing clothes around, until he started to feel a slight pain above and behind his eyes.

Darting back to the fireplace, Apple kicked at its tiles. They were at least a hundred years old and had the resistance of granite. Even if he had the right tool, the job wouldn't be an easy one.

Shooting down to one knee, Apple pulled back the heavy Turkey carpet. Underneath, there were unpainted floorboards. They looked no weaker than the tiles. But, Apple thought, there might be a loose one somewhere.

Being directly above the source of the gas, Apple had been taking in a strong dose. His stomach was complaining. The pain behind his eyes had spread to the rest of his head within the past few seconds.

Lurching away backwards in a squat, Apple took the carpet with him, exposing the boards. It needed real effort to manage the cumbersome weight. He let go when a good part of the floor had been uncovered.

One-handed, flashlight playing, Apple set about groping over the bare boards. He pressed down hard continually, seeking give. He wasn't finding any.

Apple jumped up. His panic was increasing at the same rate as the pain in his head. Testingly, he began to prance around the room on his toes like a deranged ballet dancer. That there was no one here to see him formed a smidgen of comfort.

A click sounded underfoot. Dropping, Apple pressed as hard as he could. The click came again. There was a floorboard loose. But (eyes and flashlight pin-pointing) it lay crackclose to its neighbours.

Apple rose and strode to the vanity table. He came back at once with a nail-file. This, after setting his torch down, he put into the board end, though meagerly, no more than half an inch of the metal.

He started to prise upward. The board, which was about eighteen inches wide, rose gradually and smoothly. Then, hitting proximity, it slipped free of the file and dropped back into its place.

Apple started again. This time he used the pointed end of the nail-file. When he had raised the floorboard high enough to have a lip, he held it there with his hand, dug the point in anew and went on raising.

With having to kneel, however, Apple was inhaling far more gas than he would if standing. His lungs hurt, his head was paining sharply, and he could hear in the distance that tell-tale sign of atmospheric poisoning, a metallic tap-tap-tapping.

Apple was tempted to take a break, get up and use his height to gulp at cleaner air. But that, he knew, could be the gas working its wily tricks on his rationalising. He stayed with the job.

Another half-minute, and the board came free of its neighbours. Grinning woozily, Apple flung it aside. In the shallow trench beneath lay plaster-daubed laths. It, Apple thought, was a feeble barrier.

He leapt up to his feet. The force of this in his gas-dozy condition sent him weaving away off-balance. He crashed into a rack of clothes, some of which he brought down with him as he fell onto the rolled-back carpet.

Fighting himself free, he got upright and went unsteadily back to the trench. There he raised one leg for a downward kick, but again started to lose his balance. Kneel, you idiot, he ordered himself.

He did that, the while smiling at his shrewdness. From high on one knee, he tread-kicked down on the laths. Resistance was minimal. As, widening his area, Apple kicked on repeatedly, the laths began to splinter.

This, next, caused the plaster underneath to break away. It began to fall—into, Apple realised, the baronial hall below.

Apple realised this because no sooner had an opening been made than the party's noise came up. And no sooner had the first chunks of plaster fallen than that noise changed from merry to shocked. The band stopped playing.

Ignoring the hubbub, regretting the cries of pain from those hit by falling debris, Apple kicked on without pause until all wood and plaster had been cleared from a large enough area in the trench.

Lying face down, he started to shuffle his head and shoulders through the hole to get gas-free air.

By now, the centre of the hall below was deserted, apart from debris. The guests, settled to an astonished near-silence, were staring up at what was wriggling smile-first through the hole in the ceiling.

Next morning on the location work went efficiently. Everyone was in a good mood from last night's party, which, between film talk, was the main topic of conversation.

Apple did not participate in this inquest. He was fed up with questions about the party's highlight—Tim Gordon's strange appearance above.

There had been enough of those questions at the mansion, after Apple had been pulled back up through the hole, and before he had made his exit from the house—which had been as soon as he could manage. His answers now wouldn't be any more satisfying than they had been then.

In the dressing-room Apple, still woozy, had found the lights on and the smell of gas merely faint. Not until he had finished explaining that someone had locked him in, no doubt as a joke, and that, in stumbling around by flashlight to find another way out, he must have broken the gas pipe, did he hear the other side of the story.

The lights upstairs had not been off when rescuers had come up. The door had been wide open. The gas was securely off at the main.

Everybody had to admit, however, that there was a smell of domestic gas. Which, of course, it was pointed out, could have come from what had been lying dormant in the pipes.

Apple realised what had happened. Once Clever Freddy had seen failure, as evidenced by a head appearing in the hole, he had rushed to switch the gas off, put on lights and quietly open the door. As with the car-bump flop, he was salvaging what he could by putting the blame for the incident on his victim.

Apple had realised further, from remarks and facial expressions, that everyone thought him drunk. He had exaggerated his wooziness and let them so think, offering more proof by sticking to his story despite lights and open door.

Now, lurking near a group of technicians, Apple overheard a new theory: drunk nothing, he had done it to impress Velma Wilde. This one he liked more than the other that was going the rounds: that he had been trying to upstage the stars.

Wandering on, Apple went back to the matter of perpetrator. For the dozenth time he tried to bring to mind visually the scene in the party hall, as seen from above. He wanted to know which of his suspects had been missing—busy seeing to lights and gas and door.

But Apple could recreate little of that upside-down-seeming group of starers. And in taking his hasty leave, the only person he had noticed particularly was Stan. The operative's stare had been through dead eyes.

Presently came the first of the two moments for which Apple had been waiting. Miranda Wheldon left her caravan and headed for the set. The second moment was lunch.

Apple intercepted the motion picture goddess, who headed a triangle of her courtiers. She stopped. Looking him up and down, she asked lazily, "Tried taking anything for it, darling?"

Apple joined in the chuckles before beginning on his contrite apology for last night. The Hollywood queen raised a gracious, if plump, hand. She cut in with, "Forget it, darling. That was one of the most successful parties I ever hurled. It's sure to become part of filmdom history."

"There's the matter of damage."

"The place is insured to the back teeth," Miranda Wheldon said. She waved her arm forward. "Roll, wagons." Followed by the triangle, she went on.

So that was all right, Apple thought. He wasn't surprised when, some minutes later, a grip asked him in the strictest confidence if he had been paid by the star to do his muddled Santa Claus routine.

In preparation for that second moment Apple went to the bus for the sandwiches he had hidden there, one for himself and one for Monico. They stayed hidden inside to eat; and afterwards to wait for the catering van's arrival; and last to let the serving get underway.

Apple collected his Scotch broth. He made no attempt to see who particularly was loitering near the food, apart from the three catering women. Rather, he gave all his attention to the paper cup, as though he didn't have a suspicious thought in his head.

Pretending to sip, Apple lounged away. He stood at a distance to finish his act, then moved out of sight of everyone in order to dribble broth onto the grass. After doing similarly with the ham and potato pancakes, he got milk and pear pie and headed for a quiet spot.

Into his path came Cookie. She said, "It's okay, Tim. Don't look worried."

"What?"

"I'm not going to talk about last night. These pancakes are really something."

"So's your mauve wig."

"Thanks. But listen. That Fleming character. You know, he's a jerk as well as peculiar. He has the corniest sense of humour, believe me."

"I'm willing to," Apple said. He performed a yawn, turning as he did to make sure it was seen. In an underthought he told himself that, since he was holding a plate and a cup, it was perfectly acceptable for him to not put a hand to his wide-gaping mouth.

Cookie asked, "I mean, what's funny about getting some-one's back up?"

"Nothing. But I have to run. I'm taking these to some-body."

"Who? Velma the Vamp?"

"No—Monico."

"He's right behind you, Tim."

"I know," Apple said. "But I don't want to be seen giving him people food. Some don't like that kind of thing." He walked on, telling himself, Quick thinking, Porter.

One minute later, cup and plate disposed of, Apple was lying down in a spot between two trucks. He lay face down, put his head on his arms and closed his eyes. Monico, stretch-ing out beside him, snuggled close.

Time passed. Apple kept still. All he could hear was a faint jumble of music coming from several radios. He began to make a snoring sound. Monico got up and moved away.

Apple let another ten minutes go by before cautiously rais-ing his head. Seeing no one, he got up. He was nearly at the front of the trucks, creeping, when he noticed his dog; noticed, that is, that Monico hadn't got up to follow.

Apple whispered, "Come on." Monico stayed as he was, lying with eyes closed, immobile except for his toes, which were flexing gently as though he were having a pleasant dream.

Little white cloud or tall black poodle? Apple wondered cheerfully. He was unconcerned about Monico's health (the drug was harmless) and delighted that the expected had happened. Also, for what it was worth, he now knew that the carrying agent was the Scotch broth; Monico must have stayed behind to lick up the spillage.

After giving his dog a reassuring pat, Apple went on. He left the trucks and, crouching, rounded another vehicle. There, in view of a wide area of the location, he came to a slow stop. He forgot caution. Surprise made him straighten out of his crouch like elastic being slowly stretched.

Everywhere he looked, people were asleep.

So it wasn't only Tim Gordon, Apple mused. It was the whole shooting match. And this wasn't the first time it had been tried, either. On Cavalry Stampede day there had been lots of yawners and dozers. Now, however, the drugging ploy appeared to have worked totally.

Apple went on gazing around. It was an eerie sight, with people lying still to a background of senseless music. They could have been victims of instant plague, Apple thought, or some miracle of modern warfare.

The latter gave Apple a more uncomfortable feeling than the former. Medical research could control disease, but only common sense could prevent racial suicide. Which, Apple reminded himself, was why he approved of the spy game. Anything that kept the war cold was beneficial.

Apple picked out Helen Parker, slumped in a deck-chair

with her lips in a smile; bearded Wilson Croft lying curled up on his side; the back of a mauve wig showing from under a blanket; actor-director Daniel Range flat out on an Oriental rug under his caravan's canopy.

As, cautious again, Apple began to pick his way across the location, he heard through the music a wide variety of snores, the drawl and whimper of sleep talk, what sounded like a horse being . . .

Apple stopped.

He listened acutely. The thuds could only be hoofbeats, he thought. This was proved right when now the thuds abruptly increased in rapidity—and almost at once began to grow fainter. Someone was leaving the area on horseback.

Apple began to run.

He ran hesitantly at first, but then with more sureness. Heading for the farther side of the location, he leapt over prone bodies, dodged equipment and circled vehicles.

He came to the outer rim. No radios here, he could still hear the hoofbeats. Direction was straight ahead, where rocky ground led into pine trees.

Apple looked quickly around. Not surprisingly, he was near the corral. Tethered to an outside rail were two ponies. They and the horses inside were the only creatures awake among a scattering of slumped bodies.

Apple ran to the nearest pony, a piebald. It was already saddled, to be used later in filming. Pulling the reins free, Apple threw them expertly over the animal's head as he drew it around. Horsemanship had been ignored at Damian House, but riding lessons were a Porter family tradition.

Apple leapt easily into the saddle and urged his mount away. It was sluggish. He urged it still more, and while doing so realised that, unthinkingly, he had started to use his feet. He was pushing along on the ground with his toes.

Embarrassed that his legs were that long, and glad there

were no observers, Apple nonetheless continued to pedal. He preferred it to spurring with his heels.

The piebald speeded up into a trot. Apple changed from slapping his feet down at the same time to alternating them as though in a run. He felt absurd, but it seemed to help, and the pony was carrying less weight.

They reached the rocky ground. Across it snaked a narrow sheep trail. Taking it with confidence, the pony speeded up still more. Apple helped it along with huge tiptoe strides.

They came into the pines. There was nothing to be heard now other than the noise of passage. Apple began to realise that if he couldn't hear the hoofbeats ahead, his only hope was if the horseman was seeable.

The trees went on, and on, and on. There were no signs of life anywhere. But Apple was assuming that Clever Freddy would be staying on this same trail.

They at last came out of the trees. In front lay a small vale, no longer than two football fields. At its far end, on the right, a billow of dust was lazily settling.

With a smile Apple urged his mount into greater effort. He assisted by putting even more weight on his feet. Speed increased to a gallop. Apple ran furiously.

They went over the patch of bare earth that had given up its dusty ghost, passed through a rock-sided corridor, rounded a clump of trees and came onto open land. There was nothing to be seen ahead but the diminishing trail.

They went along it.

As the minutes passed and Apple saw nothing, his confidence began to ebb. Gradually, both he and the pony eased up on their legwork. Gallop became trot, trot slipped to run, run slurred to walk.

Hoping to get lucky, to perhaps come to where the horseman had dismounted, Apple kept going. It was a quarter-hour before he realised that he was missing an opportunity.

Instead of being out here, with one chance in a hundred of scoring, he ought to be back at the location. The suspect who was not asleep there had to be Clever Freddy.

Reining in, Apple turned the pony around. He was suddenly urgent again. Reaching back while standing on tiptoe to give a good shove off, he slapped the animal's rump. The reaction was instantaneous.

Before Apple realised what was going on, the reins had slipped through his fingers and the pony had gone from between his thighs. He was left standing alone on spread-legged tiptoe.

The piebald pony trotted briskly ahead. Apple collected himself and gave running chase. He had almost caught up when the pony darted off to one side. It circled a far clump of heather, stopped there and began to graze.

Crafty, Apple went over at a walk. He hummed a Highland tune and pretended to look at the scenery. It didn't work. At the penultimate moment, the pony shied with an amused-sounding snicker and broke into a trot.

Furious, Apple followed at a run. He shouted at the stupid, rotten pigmy animal to stand bloody still for a minute. It went faster. It slowed and stopped only when its pursuer had done that first.

Three times more they went through the routine of casual, humming approach, last-minute shy and rabid chase, with Apple growing more frustrated and furious and urgent.

"To hell with it," he said finally. He set off to run back to the location. After a few yards he glanced behind. The pony was following at a pace to match his own.

Apple halted. So did the piebald.

"That's your last chance," Apple snapped. Even so, he offered other chances from time to time as he ran. The pony took none of them.

After losing his way twice, Apple came in sight of the location. He sagged in sweaty exhaustion on seeing that some people were up and about. Clever Freddy, surely, would have come back by now.

Tailed at close range by the treacherous pony, Apple trudged the final yards. Although there were still sleepers, most people were sitting or standing. On their way back from the primitive, they yawned, they stretched, they scratched their ribs like apes.

By the corral stood its keeper, Chuck Holt. He called out, "Where you been with that beast?"

Apple answered, "It got loose. I tried to get it back. It's out of its mind."

The man with the Buffalo Bill goatee lifted a blasé hand and snapped his fingers. The pony, speeding up, went straight towards the wrangler.

Disgusted, Apple veered off. But he had been close enough to note that Chuck Holt bore no obvious signs of hard riding.

Apple wandered around the location. He saw Arthur Reed talking to the script supervisor, and Wilson Croft rubbing his beard as if he had just come awake. The only person missing, Apple realised presently, was Monico.

FOUR

If Apple had made the discovery suddenly, he would no doubt have raised the alarm about his missing dog. The fact coming slowly, however, taking time to be digested, he was able to see that silence might be best, at least for the time being.

For one thing, Apple didn't want to draw that much attention to himself. Not again. Everybody would think he was some kind of fanatic. And fanatics, it might be decided, should be kept under close observation, which would curtail his activities.

Secondly, with Monico being a favourite here, people could start tramping off in all directions. There was no telling what they might find.

In the third place, this could be entirely innocent. Monico may have gone for a solo walk; or, more likely, awakening from the drugged sleep and finding his master gone, he had set off for their temporary home, the guest-house.

But Apple had little faith in the innocent. He was fairly sure that Monico had been kidnapped. Maybe Clever Freddy had seen that he was being tailed, had come straight back, and, as was his fashion, had made hay out of dead straw—by carrying the sleeping dog off somewhere.

Either the snatch was for purposes of extortion—"Play it my way if you want your dog returned alive and well"—or, again, to try and find out conclusively if Tim Gordon was straight or a counterspy.

Apple felt that Clever Freddy was not likely to do Monico

any real harm. And as for establishing the true role of his owner, Apple figured he could balk that simply by behaving as though he hadn't realised that Monico had gone.

In any case, Apple reminded himself, all this would change in about two hours. Monico was going to be needed for filming. But if the intervening shooting could be delayed . . .

Now, after checking the remainder of the vehicles which he had been covertly examining to see if Monico had accidentally been shut inside, Apple went across to the set.

As all along since the kidnapping, he wore an absent smile to show that he hadn't a care in the world. It wasn't easy to maintain. He had become less certain than formerly that Monico was in no danger.

Helen Parker, resplendent in riding costume, stood with Daniel Range in the doorway of the village inn. From the script, Apple knew that they were about to set off on a pony ride. He watched, still trying to think of a way to delay shooting—one that wouldn't make him seem even more of a madman.

The rehearsal went well. Taking the ponies from Chuck Holt, an actor-as-groom walked them into camera range and over to Helen Parker and the actor-director, both of whom made as though to mount. That was the shot. Stand-ins, filmed from behind, would do the actual mounting later, for neither Parker nor Range had a liking for horseflesh.

After another rehearsal preparations for shooting began. During this procedure, a complex affair, Apple came up with a decent idea.

He circled to where the ponies would be facing. There, in a spot where behind him was no one who had an interest in the filming, he sank to a squat.

Soon came the ritual calls:

"Let's have quiet, please."

"Everyone but principals off the set."

"This is a take we're doing here."

"Settle down, please."

"Put that bloody cigarette out, the smoke's drifting over."

"All okay now."

"Take one."

"Action!"

The actor-groom came forward with his pair of ponies. He stopped by the two stars. At that, Apple got up silently. The piebald saw him. It flicked its head high. Daniel Range said a drab "Cut."

Apple was already on his way back down to a squat. No one, he saw, had noticed his movements. He would have felt smug if he hadn't been so worried about Monico.

They did the take twice more with similar results—Apple rising and the pony flicking its head. However, as the piebald's response had grown less pronounced each time, Apple knew that soon it would stop reacting altogether.

But he got lucky. Before the calls began for take four, Helen Parker turned to Daniel Range with a cross "Why do we have to do this stupid shot anyway?"

"What do you mean?"

"The stand-ins could do the whole thing."

The actor-director said dismissingly, "Don't be ridiculous, angel."

The supporting actress dropped her riding-crop. "Daniel," she said coldly, "no one has ever thought me an angel, and no one has ever called me ridiculous."

Apple didn't wait to hear the rest of it. Congratulating himself on the success of his ploy, he got up and left the set area. He put on his show smile. It hurt.

So that no one would notice the absence of Monico at his side, Apple sat in the guest-house bus. He was relieved, but not surprised, when later an assistant director came to say that the dog's scenes would have to be put off until morning.

Apple stayed in the bus, although moving to the rear seat. And, when back at the guest-house, he kept to it until everyone else had got off, although he was itching to rush in search of Monico.

Giving whistles that could be construed by the casual listener as part of a tune, Apple walked around the building. Nothing. He went inside and up to his room. Empty.

So now it was definite, Apple thought as he flopped back onto the bed. Monico had been snatched. Next would come a note or telephone call.

Apple wondered how he was going to handle the extortion. Which, in fine, would he put first—the caper or the safety of his dog?

Apple didn't wonder for long. He shied from the question like that pony.

But, of course, Apple thought, there was always a chance of getting a lead on Monico's whereabouts. Perhaps with another look around, or with a few discreet questions. Or was it better to wait here until contacted?

Half an hour later Apple, still debating the matter, heard a slithery sound. He froze. Knowing what the sound must signify, he lay still until it had ended. He leapt off the bed and stooped to grab up the piece of paper that had been slid under the door.

He mangled it open. It was tomorrow's call-sheet.

Glum, Apple left the room. He told himself cheerlessly to be of good cheer. Clever Freddy would do Monico no harm. After all, his mother had been half-English.

On the stairs Apple met Bill, the injured prop-man. After they had agreed about the classic quality of this afternoon's row between Helen Parker and Daniel Range, Apple ventured: "You haven't seen Monico around, have you?"

"You've lost him?"

"Oh no. We're playing hide-and-seek."

"You're a real character," Bill laughed, going on up briskly. "That ceiling routine. Blimey."

Brilliant start, Porter, Apple thought as he descended. He went back behind the stairs and outside via the rear door. After a repeat examination of an outbuilding, he strode around to the car park.

The only person there was a suspect, Apple recognised from the green coverall. Gardener McKay, bending beside his pedal bicycle, was pumping up the tyre beneath the carrier's weight of a bulky sack.

As Apple hesitated, the crew-cut gardener looked around, saw him and slowly straightened. Smiling, he asked in his guttural Scots, "How's your winter roses?"

"Ah," Apple said. "Fine." He nodded. He didn't know what to say next. He had become confused with all the he-knows and I-knows, if McKay should be Clever Freddy.

The gardener asked, "Would ye like a couple of crocus bulbs?" He nudged the sack. "Got plenty here."

Still in the cloud of his confusion, Apple backed away. "No, thanks," he said. "I haven't had dinner yet." Aware of McKay's puzzled expression, he turned and quickly retraced his steps. The loss of Monico, he realised, was affecting his cool as well as his processes of rationalisation.

By the back door Apple stopped and got out a cigarette. He could see that he was going to get nowhere with discreet questions, or by continuing to pretend that Monico wasn't missing. All he could do was wait for contact.

He lit up, thinking that only one thing was certain: Monico wouldn't be returned until he had served Clever Freddy's purpose. Which could mean days. So, to be fair to the film company, it should be reported that the dog-actor was missing.

And the one to report this fact to, Apple realised, was another suspect: production chief Arthur Reed. If nothing else, Reed's response would be interesting.

As Apple dropped his cigarette and ground it out, he knew he had the answer to his previous question, of which came first, dog or mission. Sighing at his lack of professionalism, he admitted that he would rather see the caper fall apart than have Monico hurt. Friends came before country.

"Yes, you may go up, sir," said the man at the reception desk of the King's Messenger as he put down his in-house telephone. "Suite seven."

Apple crossed to the lift. He didn't make the effort of looking around to see if his fair-haired colleague Rex was on the premises—and an observer of this trespass. He had no concern to spare for matters of that feeble nature.

Up on the top floor Apple went towards the door which was standing open. He smoothed down his hair. It was still damp from the fast shower he had taken before his equally fast drive to town. He was agitated under an exterior of calm.

Apple kept on going inside at a call to enter. He closed the door behind him. "Good evening."

"Good evening, Tim. Call me Arthur."

"I know."

"That's right," the production man said. Standing in the centre of an elegant sitting room, he had the perfect backdrop for his ensemble of silk robe, neck scarf and poised glass of champagne.

He spread a soft hand over his drink to ask, "May I get you something?"

"No, thanks," Apple said. "It's not a social call. I'm afraid I've come with bad news." He was watching closely.

"Bad news?"

"Monico is missing."

Arthur Reed frowned as though he had a slight pain. "Is she the girl with . . . um . . . ?"

"Monico is my dog. And he's missing."

The pain hovered. "I'm not sure that I know what you mean. The dog's run away?"

"Possibly," Apple said. "Or wandered off and got lost. All I know is, I discovered him gone at the location but thought he'd headed for home. He hadn't. He's missing."

"I see," Arthur Reed said briskly, free of pain. "Then I suppose you had better inform the police."

"Is that what you advise?"

"Well, that's what one usually does with lost articles, so I understand."

"I can't go to the authorities anyway," Apple said. "I brought my dog into this country from Ibiza without him doing the usual six months in quarantine as a precaution against rabies."

"Isn't that illegal?"

"Highly. Rabies doesn't exist here in the land of dog worshippers. They'd put me in prison and throw the key away."

"Then I don't know what advice to give," Arthur Reed said, raising the champagne glass to his lips. Finding it empty, he put it behind his back. "Sorry."

"You don't get the message," Apple said. He felt outclassed and more agitated. "Monico is going to be needed, tomorrow morning and for some days after, for filming. He isn't here. He is not available. Shooting will have to be postponed."

The pain came back to the well-massaged face, at its original slightness to begin with, but then growing steadily until it was a grinding ache. Bringing his glass front and holding it in both hands like a beggar's bowl, Arthur Reed came across the room.

He asked, "Do you realise what this production is costing per diem?"

"I can imagine."

"A fortune, that's what. And we're already behind schedule.

More so because of that foolish argument today. This cannot happen."

"It already has."

"Oh."

"Sorry," Apple said. "It's not my fault."

Arthur Reed looked up at him steadily. If this was a performance, Apple mused, it deserved an Oscar. But, of course, a performance it was, even though Reed might not be Clever Freddy: the production man playing to the hilt the career role he had worked so hard to win.

"All right," Arthur Reed said firmly, his pain weakening. "We won't go into faults. Not at the moment. The thing to do is get back that dog. Agreed?"

"One hundred per cent."

"And it can be done. We'll find him, don't worry on that score. You just let me know tomorrow morning, first thing, if the dog's still missing. Then we'll get to work." He went around Apple and opened the door. "We can't fail."

"Fail at what?"

"At a good scouring," Arthur Reed said. "That's the way to do it, on a large scale." He started to usher Apple through the doorway. "A crowd scene, as it were."

"I don't get you, Arthur."

"I'll have a hundred people out there searching. Two hundred. Three. Never mind the wildlife. We'll find that dog in no time flat. Good night, Tim. I'll be expecting your call." He finished his ushering and closed the door.

Apple stood for a moment before starting to walk slowly away. He nodded in order to encourage himself to accept the truth: that there were going to be hundreds of people tramping over the estate. One of them could easily come across the laboratory. And it would all be the fault of Appleton Porter—through the good offices of Clever Freddy.

So, Apple thought, Arthur Reed couldn't be the free lance spy. Unless this was a bluff. But to gain what?

Dismissing that, Apple told himself he had to assume for now that Arthur Reed was all that he was trying to seem. Which meant that he had to be stopped from sending out that massive search party. How?

Obviously, Apple thought, there was no sense in going back with some story to explain why Tim Gordon didn't want his dog found. There had to be a way for Monico to *be* found. But that, the answer to everything, would need a stroke of genius.

Brilliance, Apple amended, nervous of the ultimate. Or anyway, extra smartness. He had to out-clever the undoubtedly clever Clever Freddy. The matter needed to be given some powerful thought. At once.

With assistance in mind, Apple quickened his step.

The snack-bar, sole business still open around the town square, was empty apart from staff. These two girls, late teens, wore expressions of boredom—which, Apple thought, were probably to hide the fact that they were bored.

The girls brightened when the tall customer entered. He, they obviously guessed, was part of the film unit, those fascinating movie people who led glamorous lives and did super, super things. The girls looked across the counter expectantly, alert, ready for anything.

With a distant awkwardness at sitting while females were on their feet, Apple took a stool. He asked, "Do you have any lemon marmalade?"

The girls stared; winced; nodded.

"Good. I'll have some on toast, please. And I'd like a pot of tea." He smiled apologetically.

"Yes, sir," the girls murmured, dull. They moved away at a sluggish pace to get the order.

Which was Apple's favourite snack, as well as the brain

food that he found the most effective. Never had he ventured to suggest to himself that his increased mental ability might come from the sugar. He didn't want to spoil the mystique.

The order was served. Apple paid. After preparing and sipping a cup of tea, to start the rite off, he picked up the first slice of marmaladed toast. He began to eat.

Ignoring the glances of reproach from the two girls, crunching gladly, Apple acknowledged that as far as he was concerned there was no stand-in for marmalade with the flavour of lemon.

An idea came on crunch three.

What he could do, Apple told himself, was try finding a substitute for Monico. All Ibizan hounds looked pretty much alike and were easy to get along with. It was neat except for two points, even forgetting the shortness of time: the dog most likely wouldn't be trained, and in Scotland that breed of hound would be scarcer than kilts. Forget it.

Apple had stopped chewing, had been rigid-faced throughout the foregoing cogitation. This, he realised, had been noted by his audience, which was watching him tensely.

Apple chewed on. The girls relaxed and exchanged looks from under heavy eyelids.

Slice one finished, Apple drank more tea. He lifted and bit into the second slice of toast. Judiciously, he agreed that he wouldn't be lying if he said that this one had more character than the other.

Many torpid, steady crunches passed before Apple got the next possible solution. He went on chewing while giving it a good mulling over.

He could always lie to Arthur Reed in the morning, Apple acknowledged. He could say that Monico had come back safe and sound. That would give him another couple of hours, a pause to allow more time for the try at coming up with something. It might be worth the trouble.

Apple went on considering this until he became aware that he had been chewing the same mouthful of toast for rather a long time. Flicked glances showed him that his audience was watching closely.

He swallowed and placed the last bit of slice two into his mouth. Masticating steadily, he closed his eyes the better to concentrate. There was no sound in the snack-bar other than the crunching.

Apple stopped his jaw movements to play with the notion of reporting Arthur Reed's search plan to the administrators of the Glengael estate. They, hopefully, would step in and call a halt to the scheme.

On the other hand, Apple thought, they might be sympathetic, and not only acquiesce but throw in a score or two of extra searchers. Scrub it.

Apple crunched on and swallowed. In reaching, eyes still closed, for the third slice of toast, he put his fingertips in its marmalade.

Eyes open but directed down, Apple licked his fingers. He made a thorough job of it, sensing meanwhile that the girls had moved closer, one on either side.

Apple realised what a disappointment he must be to them. They would have been expecting great excitements from the presence of a motion picture company, and must have been badly let down, seeing almost nothing of the early-to-work, early-to-bed movie people. Now one of those people sat right here and he was just like the man next door, except for height. The girls were no doubt losing hope of seeing something unusual before the company left.

Apple upbraided himself for letting his mind wander from the important task in hand. Was the recovery of Monico of so little consequence?

Sternly, Apple lifted the third slice of toast. He put it in his mouth corner first, and bit. At once he got an idea. It was so good that he forgot about chewing. He stayed like that, staring ahead, the toast in his mouth and his jaw motionless.

Apple turned the idea over and around. He squeezed it inside out. He ran it from back to front like a palindrome. He put it slowly through the wringer. He stood away for a cool appraisal.

Throughout these trials, Apple remained unaware of his facial contortions. His immersion in thought was total. As he gradually became more stimulated, the piece of toast began to twitch and jerk.

The idea was genuinely good, Apple concluded. It stood an excellent chance of working. And if it did, every immediate problem would be solved.

Arousing himself perkily, Apple bit off the corner and put the rest of the slice down. Brain food time was over. He swallowed, slapped his hands on the counter and rose.

"Thank you," he said. "Thank you very much. Thank you very much indeed."

Turning, he strode quickly to the door and went out, his gaze already on the telephone-box in the square. Before reaching the kerb he realised that he needed change. He swung around and hurried back into the snack bar.

The girls had moved to stand side by side. Apple, not wishing to ask for change by itself, which was poor form, said, "A box of matches, please."

By shaking their heads and gesturing, the girls signified that matches were not on sale here. One said, "But I can give you some."

"No, thank you," Apple said. "I have a lighter." He was looking around with keen eyes. Suddenly, he laughed, pointing. "Those sugar-buns." They would be ideal for Monico's sweet tooth.

The other girl said, "They're stale, sir. Three days old at least. Sorry."

"That's just fine," Apple said. "Lovely. I'll take two, please. Do you happen to have a noisy bag to put them in?" Monico was a one for his crackly bags.

The girls slowly shook their heads like the worried at an auction, at the same time inching closer together.

"Well, never mind," Apple said. "They'll do as they are."

Eagerly, he leaned his tall trunk over the counter, stretched out a long arm to a shelved plate, scooped up two of the buns. He put them in his pockets after straightening.

While the girls were making change, both going to the till, Apple paused in his eagerness to sympathise with their evaporating hopes. He wished he could help. He wondered if he ought to do or say something that would give at least a dram of satisfaction: a strange remark, or some kind of odd behaviour.

Until the girls came with his change, Apple toyed with ideas. Nothing of value emerged. Deciding against creative assistance—another bite of marmaladed toast, which would look peculiar—he took his coins and went to the door, where he came to an abrupt halt.

What if, Apple thought carefully, he were to take that same piece of toast, reach up and stick it on the ceiling? Surely, that would knock them out.

He turned with a grin to face the girls. But he knew immediately that he couldn't go through with it. And he insisted to himself that courage had nothing to do with this. It was just that he was beginning to have a thing about ceilings. It had to be nipped in the bud.

With a shrug of apology, Apple turned away again. He went outside and headed across the square, sighing. He hated to let people down.

It was a one-minute task to telephone the guest-house and get its new gardener's home number. Now it was that number which Apple dialled in the telephone-box, whose door he was keeping ajar with a foot because of his claustrophobia.

"Hello, Mr. McKay," he said when a familiar, guttural voice answered. "This is Tim Gordon. Remember me?"

"The tall laddie?"

"That's right. I'm calling you because we'll probably be moving on tomorrow, and I wanted to thank you for your advice on those winter roses."

The gardener asked sharply, "Moving on?"

"Afraid so," Apple said with resignation. "You see, my dog's disappeared. I suspect criminals of being responsible. You know, some crooks specialise in snatching rare or expensive dogs and holding them for ransom."

"Aye, I've heard of it."

"Well, I'm not going to pay. It's against my principles. So, as the filming can't go on without Monico, the company is planning to leave. *If,* that is, Monico hasn't been found by tomorrow morning early. But between you and me, I'm not really hoping for anything. I think I've lost my dog."

The gardener began to condole. Apple cut in with a drear voice, thanked him again and disconnected. As he left the box, he told himself that if McKay was Clever Freddy, he would now start to worry about his cover job: if the motion picture company left, the proprietress of Blancairn might let her new gardener go.

Apple continued on across the town square. Circumspectly, he entered the hotel. Its pop lobby was as crowded as usual. Clearly visible in the middle was a black stetson. Apple could also see Rex, who stood behind the bar washing glasses. The operative didn't look happy.

Chuck Holt was facing the other way, sitting at a table with other film people. Apple knew that if he were to go around in order to catch his eye, agent Rex would see. He would have to wait for Holt to turn.

Ten minutes was enough. Apple went to a cowl-type public telephone nearby. He had to stoop to fit. From the slim directory he got the King's Messenger's number, which he dialled. From across the lobby, he was both able to see and hear the reception-desk clerk who answered.

In the terse tones of emergency, Apple said he wanted to have Mr. Holt paged. The clerk looked around, saw the black hat and sent a page-boy over. Nodding with indifference, the wrangler got up. He slouched to the desk and picked up the telephone.

"So what's the strife?" he asked.

"This is Tim Gordon," Apple said. "I thought I'd better warn you to be careful."

"Me? Careful?"

"There's a gang of rustlers in these here parts. They've pinched my dog, and could be they're after your horses. If I were you, I'd stand guard tonight. From tomorrow it won't matter so much."

Chuck Holt looked at the receiver, put it back to his face and asked, "What is all this? Rustlers in Scotland? And whatcha mean, it won't matter tomorrow?"

"No time for details. This is all secret anyway. But what it boils down to is this: if I don't get my dog back by morning, the film company's going to use that as an excuse to pull out of the region. There's insurance money involved. All a bit crafty-dirty. Anyway, we leave the location tomorrow—if Monico doesn't show up. Keep an eye on those horses, eh? So long." He disconnected.

Slowly, Chuck Holt put down the receiver. He stood there for a moment before turning away and aiming back for his table. His expression was pensive.

If the wrangler was Clever Freddy, Apple thought in satisfaction, he would be seeing that, if Monico didn't get released, his freedom to come and go on the Glengael estate was finished. He would either have to quit, or start again from scratch with a new cover.

Apple would have liked to stay on with his head in the cowl, to see what, if anything, Chuck Holt did, but he had business to attend to back at the guest-house. He sidled out to the square.

Some minutes later he was parking his van beside other vehicles at Blancairn. He strode inside briskly. The first person who caught his eye in the lobby was Cookie. She was sitting with a book.

It occurred to Apple that it might be better if the threat of mass departure were given a little wider circulation. After all, Clever Freddy might not be one of the suspects. Therefore, if someone who liked gossip . . .

Going across, Apple let himself sink tiredly down beside the woman in the chartreuse wig. After an exchange of hellos he said, "I have no right to tell you this."

The book almost slipped from Cookie's hands. "If you don't," she said, "I'll throw myself off an armchair."

Apple looked behind, sank his head, lowered his voice. "You mustn't breathe a word," he said. "Not one. But it looks as if the job here ends tomorrow." He explained about Monico's criminal kidnapping. "Since I'm not paying, no way is this going to be a short-term operation."

Cookie was staring at him in surprise. "But they can simply delay shooting, or shoot around Monico—poor darling."

Apple shook his head. "That's the crux of all this. The company bosses want to quit here. Monico gives them the perfect excuse. They have an excellent reason, which I can't go into at the moment."

Cookie nodded. "Okay."

"But it's so good a reason that one might even suspect Monico's disappearance of being . . . never mind." He began to get to his feet. "All I do know for sure is that unless my dog comes back, we fold. But not a word."

"Don't worry," Cookie said, still staring. "I won't even breathe a comma."

"Thanks. See you."

Moving toward the entrance to the bar, in search of his next prospect, Apple told himself that an interested party would be moved to Monico-returning action by Cookie's story, while the disinterested would treat it as just another of those location rumours that the retired stunt-person was always peddling around.

Before he had a chance to look in the bar, Apple saw the man he sought. Near-uniformed Wilson Croft was going into the dining-room. Apple followed.

He followed as far as the glass doors. He halted there on seeing that Croft was about to join others at a table. Apple moved back to a chair to wait.

The wait was long. Apple almost fell asleep after he had made the mistake of reminding himself that he'd had a long, busy day. He was biting off a yawn when at last the bearded security man appeared, alone.

Apple got up quickly and intercepted him. He said, solemn, "I've a good mind to report you to your employers. Fine security you provide."

Putting fists to hips, Wilson Croft said, "What the hell're you talking about?"

Wrapped in a charge of dereliction of duty, Apple first gave his news of his dog's criminal disappearance. He allowed Croft to have his hot, defensive say before going on with the end-to-filming story. He hinted with nods and winks at several strange, secret reasons.

Wilson Croft folded his arms to ask, "And they'll really pull up stakes?"

"If Monico isn't found, yes. They'll use what they already

have in the can of his work. But I think we'll all be glad to leave, what with all those peculiar goings-on."

"That's as may be. But as far as my security's concerned—"

"Good night," Apple said, moving away. He went straight across to the stairs, where he began to climb.

On rounding onto the second flight, he came upon Johnny Fleming, who was leaning on the wall, and who said, "Thought you'd sit there for ever."

"So did I."

"What's to this story I've heard, about the dog and the quitting? Sounds like rubbish."

"The first part isn't. Monico's gone. The rest of it you can forget. It's imaginary."

Johnny Fleming said, "That's what I thought."

"The truth is that Arthur Reed's going to swamp the area of the location with searchers tomorrow. They'll find the lab, more than likely. And so, therefore, will Clever Freddy. But it won't do him any good. Secrecy gone, the laboratory will have to be moved. Thus a great spot's been ruined. It's a loss for everybody."

"I was getting to like this job. There's a make-up girl who fancies me."

Going on by: "Good night."

"Sorry about the dog."

"Thanks," Apple said, glancing back with the word as he went up the stairs. He plodded to his room.

The following hours lacked charm. With the light off in hopes of not discouraging callers, pacing was difficult. Apple reluctantly gave it up after stubbing his toes on a piece of furniture. He tried various positions.

He sat, lay, stood, knelt, squatted, leaned. Lying down was best, but he had to do it on the floor, the bed being too conducive to sleep; and even then he needed to be both on his side so as to avoid looking at the ceiling, and to be on guard against telling himself what a long, busy day he'd had.

At one o'clock in the morning, sure that if he didn't move he would begin to froth at the mouth, Apple silently left his room. At once he felt less tired, and at twice he realised that there was still one ploy he hadn't tried. Though on the feeble side, it was a hope.

Apple went down through the silent, dimly lit house. He made an exit by the front, that being the least suspicious. There was a mist.

Turning right, Apple went to the corner. He moved away from it some yards, but not too far (Monico, after all, could be hidden inside), and came to a stop.

After looking carefully all around through the mistiness, Apple cleared his throat, raised his head—and barked. The bark was short and followed by two more of the same ilk. His hope was that he would hear the answer of a familiar yelp.

He heard nothing.

Apple went around to the other three points of the house. At each, he gave the triple bark. The result was negative.

Chilled by the cold and emotions, his tiredness in charge again, Apple returned indoors and went upstairs. When he got back to his room, he found the map.

Lights switched on, Apple calmed with a cigarette before giving the piece of paper his close attention, and after seeing that it was what he had been waiting for.

He paced and smoked and looked at the ceiling openly and congratulated himself on his shrewdness in going out of the room in order to give Clever Freddy the chance to make a safe visit. He didn't smoke his cigarette the whole way through.

The map, drawn in ball-point on cheap paper, showed Glengael's gate, a winding path inside the estate, and a cave. One arrow pointing to the cave had as feathers, in a childish print, DOG; a second, shooting at the path, had ONE MILE.

Making no mental comment on the possibility of trickery, Apple hurried into a warm topcoat. He left his room, left the house, went to his van. After checking that the flashlight in the glove compartment was working efficiently, he started the motor and drove off.

The early-hours road was deserted. Apple could have gone at whatever speed the Austin was capable of, but he was held to caution by the mist, which, prospects being good, he enjoyed for its romantic aspect rather than cursed as a delayer.

When he judged from landmarks that he had about a furlong to go to the gate, Apple steered off onto open land. After rounding clumps of heather, he stopped with the road no longer visible—meaning, more to the point, that his van wasn't visible from the road.

He got out with his flashlight. Beam leading the way, he set off walking at a smart stride.

This Apple changed to a run on nearing where the pigpen lay on the other side of Glengael's wall. He didn't slow again until he had climbed the padlocked gate and left the putrid smell behind.

The path underfoot was like hundreds of others which crisscrossed the estate. That it was the right one showed by the rock formations that were duplicated on the man. At least Apple told himself so. Nothing could be absolute when working from a crude sketch, as well as among surroundings rendered vague by the mistiness and deceptive by the beam of the flashlight.

Apple had almost a mile to go, according to information. He travelled at a steady trot. He tried to use time to gauge the distance he covered, reckoning on eight minutes to do a mile at his present pace.

From the rocks and heather on either hand, as well as from

the pine trees, came furtive sounds: slitherings, scurryings, chirps and squeaks. It was sinister company. Apple was glad to be hurrying.

The eight minutes soon passing, he began to walk; also to look about more actively for the tower of rock under which, the map said, the cave could be found. He hoped he hadn't travelled too far.

The rock tower failed to appear, though twice, his heart twitching, Apple was fooled by trees. He halted. Lifting his head, he barked. There was nothing in reply. He went on a dozen yards and barked again.

This time he heard—or seemed to hear—a cry with a dog-like pitch.

It had come from his left. He plunged through heather in that direction, leaving the path behind. The thought came to him that he might get lost. And stay so. It wasn't uncommon in the Highlands, where sometimes hikers died from exposure in foul weather.

It wasn't his safety, however, that Apple was concerned about. What bothered him was the idea of being responsible for a mammoth search—police, soldiers, volunteers, helicopters.

Ignoring that, Apple waded on through the heather. He stopped in a clear patch, where he barked loudly, nine or ten times. In return, he heard a single, shrill, questioning yelp whose ownership was unmistakable.

"Monico!" Apple shouted.

He ran off to his right. Which, he judged, was taking him back to the path. He reached it at the same time as his flashlight beam picked out the tower of rock. It was straight ahead.

Giving one bark and two shouts, all answered with yelps, Apple went on at an untidy run. He arrived at the pinnacle, saw its triangle-shaped entrance, stumbled at a stoop inside the cave behind the light beam, saw his dog and gave a final, triumphant shout.

It was a joyful reunion. There would have been more physical action out of Monico, who gasped and spluttered, had it not been that he was leashed closely with rope to a stake in the ground.

By the time he was untied by slow, unsteady fingers, he had settled, accepting the fact of rescue. It took Apple a little longer. While asking Monico repeatedly how he was, then, and feeding him the two buns, he smoked a cigarette down to the filter.

They left the cave. In his pocket Apple had the length of old, hairy rope; he might come across some more to match it. He was sorry that he had thoughtlessly not taken any notice of the knots; they might have told him something.

With Monico staying close behind him, Apple went back along the path. The chill air soon had him going at a run. Monico's enjoyment of the pace was no greater than his own.

Apple had no worries about getting lost. The reverse. He grew so confident that when he judged himself in relation to time to be a couple of furlongs from the gate, knowing that the way there was fairly straight, he decided to cut a corner. He would head diagonally for where he had left his van.

Although pathless, the going was reasonably smooth, with the land level and the heather in shy patches. Apple was able to make excellent time.

With complacency, however, his tiredness began to come back. Soon he slowed to a walk. He mused that he would be glad when he was in bed so he could freely reflect on what a long, busy day he'd had.

Apple was passing quietly through a copse of mist-shrouded trees when he heard the sound. It was a click.

Apple stopped walking. He was bumped into by Monico, with whom, turning, he then shared a glance; neither learned anything. The click came again. Apple switched off his flashlight.

Because of the white mist, visibility was reasonably good. Apple could see shapes and shadows. What he couldn't see as, peering, he swung in a slow circle, was anything to connect with that metallic clicking.

Which sounded again now.

Apple jerked his head about. It did no good. Direction was impossible to figure. But the noise had seemed close at hand, a matter of yards.

Experiencing the eeriness of the situation, Apple allowed himself to shiver. He wondered if he had walked into an ambush. Yet that was ridiculous, he thought. Was Clever Freddy so brilliant that he had expected the short-cutting? Or had he been following all this time, just waiting to catch up in the right place.

The second was possible, Apple knew. Sinking to a low semi-crouch, he went cautiously and silently on. He held the dark flashlight as if it were a weapon. When he heard the voice, he stumbled, for he was caught between wanting to halt and wanting to keep going.

The voice was a chuckle. Although it wasn't strong enough to give away if its maker was adult or child, male or female, the low laugh did give the impression of evil. Which, Apple told himself severely, was due to the ambience.

Unstumbling, he decided in favour of continued motion. Ambience or not, he didn't like sinister laughs when they came in conjunction with clicks that could be from firearms. Nor did he like trouble when he was with Monico.

Switching the flashlight's beam on again, ending his caution, Apple began to barge through the trees. He was noisy, clattering branches and heather. Even so, he still heard the voice. A wordless cry, it was raised as if in warning.

It was followed by two clicks.

Apple raced on without finesse, like a bag-snatcher. He was pleased to own long legs. He crashed through undergrowth, pounded his shoes down heavily, worked hard at keeping the beam of his torch steady on the way ahead.

While Apple had no intentions of lessening the racket he was making, in order to hear if there were sounds of chase, this came about by accident when he entered a glade. Its thick turf had him springing lightly and silently.

There were no chase sounds. There was no sound at all from behind, save for Monico's panting.

Apple went on with less frenzy.

He was neither ashamed of himself for running away, nor abject at having maybe missed a chance of catching Clever Freddy. Even discounting the danger, that he had got Monico back safely was event enough for the time being. And he wanted to keep him safe.

Reminding himself that he could return here tomorrow and snoop for clues, Apple continued at a lope until he came to the estate wall.

That climbed, he was five minutes finding the van, another six getting back to Blancairn, a further two reaching his room, and a final one undressing and sliding into bed, where he told himself he most certainly had had a long, busy . . .

Thirty seconds later, or so it seemed, the telephone was screeching at him.

Apple came grudgingly awake to answer. But it wasn't his wake-up call. The desk said that shooting was off: the mist had strengthened.

After arranging for an all-clear message to be delivered later to Arthur Reed, Apple went gratefully back to sleep.

FIVE

Apple slept until noon. His dog had not been so unoccupied, he found on finally getting out of bed. A scattering of fibres on the floor told that, after taking from the overcoat pocket that length of tethering rope, Monico had chewed it to total destruction.

Apple didn't mind clearing up the mess. He knew about the sweetness of revenge—as well as its bitter after-taste. What did annoy him was that Monico hadn't chewed the rope before, in the cave, to free himself. But it fitted with all that Apple had learned about Ibizan hounds; they were weak on intellect, strong on emotion.

Apple showered and dressed. After a stroll outdoors in the mist (during which he saw nothing of gardener McKay), he took Monico into the dining-room. They ate well, visited briefly meanwhile by several of the other guests.

Most of them said with a knowing nod how good it was to see the old fellow again. Wilson Croft merely grunted, "It's back, evidently." Cookie fussed over Monico between assurances that the secret had been safe with her, sort of, in a manner of speaking.

The retired stunt person added, "We're getting a poker game together. You wanna join in?"

Apple declined with thanks. He had been thinking that there was no time like the present, the perfect misty present, to do a bit of investigating at that place where he had heard the voice and clicks.

Leaving the table as soon as he had finished his meal, eager to start, Apple went to the glass doors. When through them he paused on seeing Velma Wilde.

The bit player sat in the chair where Apple had waited yesterday for Wilson Croft. Velma was half-way through a yawn, which she quickly snarled off as she rose.

Coming straight to Apple with her over-slinky walk, she looked up at him and said in the off-key tones of reproach, "You've been neglecting me."

Apple blinked, shook his head, crackled the wax in his ears. He said, "I'm sorry, I didn't quite catch that."

"You, Tim, have been neglecting me disgracefully."

"I still didn't quite—"

Velma Wilde said poutingly, "You haven't looked at me once lately, nor have you spoken a word."

Apple blinked again, accepting that there was nothing wrong with his hearing. "I haven't?"

"No, Tim. You're the only one around here with any real charm, and I've missed it since you gave up taking notice of me."

Fumblingly, Apple protested that he had never stopped admiring her from afar, that he thought she was a sensationally attractive girl, that his charm, such as it was, was hers for the asking whenever she felt in need of it, at dawn or midnight.

"That's just darling."

"Really?"

Back to pouting, Velma Wilde took his arm. "But I think you owe me a drink to make up for your neglect."

"Of course," Apple said. He was dazed, but smiling at the way his luck seemed to be changing all around. "I am yours to command, Miss Wilde."

"Velma, dear."

They crossed the lounge and went into the bar. Apple stayed mostly in his smiling daze during the ordering of drinks from a waiter, their arrival and the reduction of their levels to the minimum.

Only when the subject of a second round was broached by his companion did Apple realise (1) that they were sitting at a corner table holding hands, and (2) that he had just drunk gin, which he disliked. It made him smell like a presser in a dry-cleaner's.

"I'll just have a soft drink," Apple said. "I'm thirsty. But you have another, if you want."

She did want. She wanted strongly enough to order a double, which, when the drinks came, she sank swiftly, in one shot. Apple belched quietly for her.

Velma squeezed his hand. She said, snuggling close and gazing up at him, "I'll never forget when you saved me from those wild stallions. Jesus."

Apple told himself so while he was telling the bit player that it was nothing, nothing at all.

"Are you serious, Tim? Not many would've done that."

"Any man who isn't prepared to risk his life for a gorgeous lady ought to be shot."

"There it is," Velma Wilde said. "Charm." Since she was unable to get any closer with her snuggle, she shivered. "You've got gallons of it."

"Oh, I don't know."

"It's as true as my glass is empty."

"Would you like some pink champagne?" Apple asked. He was still overwhelmed at being called charming. No one had ever called him that before, except his mother, and she, he had early realised, was prone to exaggeration.

Apple quickly stopped thinking about his mother when he heard a warm "No, Tim, on second thoughts I'd like you to see me upstairs."

"Um . . . now?"

"Right this very minute."

Apple's next settled, concrete awareness was of being in a bedroom. It was similar to his own. On their way here, it appeared, they had left Monico off.

Velma drew the drapes at the mist-white window, saying, "Let's keep this dreary weather out."

After clearing his throat in the gloom, Apple suggested switching on a lamp. The hostess compromised by putting on the bathroom light and leaving the door open a crack. She sat her guest in the bedroom's only chair.

Apple got out cigarettes. Working hard at sophistication, he put two in his mouth. He lit them and handed one to Velma, the while giving a prolonged wink, which eased the smoke sting in his eye.

Velma stood facing him and beside the bed. With her hands on the hips of her shiny blue dress, she heeled off one shoe and then the other.

Apple said it was a nice place she had here.

In a low, intimate tone, which went agreeably with the room's subdued lighting, Velma said, "There's something different about you, Tim."

"Well, I don't know about that," Apple mumbled, shy. The last thing in his mind was the caper and his cover.

"I mean it. Really different."

"Let's not talk about me, Velma. Not when you're here. You're far more interesting."

"Not yet I'm not," the bit player said calmly. "It'll take a while before I establish myself big in movies, before people recognize that I have star quality. I'm going to be great."

"You are. I know it."

"Would you hold this, please?"

Leaning forward, Apple took the cigarette from Velma. With so much mental comment going on that his mind was a jumble, he watched her reach behind to unfasten catches.

Hands front again she pulled the blue dress forward. It fell to the floor and she footed it aside.

Apple's tobacco-auction mind came through with a bid at one clear thought: What a good thing it was that Monico had been left elsewhere.

Arms akimbo again, Velma stood statuesque in her shiny black briefs and the matching bra that was bearing up well considering the pressure involved. She had one of those sideways navels that seem to be smiling.

In her intimate voice she said, "It's not just that you're sensitive and charming, Tim dear. You're completely different from any of the other movie people around here. Or anywhere else, for that matter."

"Precisely," Apple murmured. His mind jumbled on, and not one of those busy thoughts was connected with the mission or the phony dog-handler.

"I can't quite put my finger on it, Tim."

"Okay."

Again Velma put her hands behind. She bent forward, her long hair swaying. When she straightened up, the black bra came free with a leap. It shot down her arms and off, landing neatly on a bedpost. Velma posed.

Through the smoke curling up from the two cigarettes he was holding, Apple stared one-eyed at the magnificent bosom. It was one of the proudest he had ever seen, he managed to think. After which he wondered if, to be fair and decent, he ought to tell Velma the truth about horses. And after that, he quickly sent his mind back to an outpost in the jumble.

"That prop-man called Fleming," Velma said. "He's also like an outsider, come to think of it."

"Absolutely," Apple whispered.

"But let's not talk about others."

"You're right."

"In fact," Velma said, her voice growing even more intimate and her eyes looking sleepy, "let's not talk at all."

Apple gave a sort of nod. "Certainly." He had only a faint idea of what he was saying.

Velma Wilde hooked dainty fingers inside her briefs, which she coaxed down until they were able to do a free fall. Naked, she stepped across to where Apple sat, his watching eye throbbing. After taking back her cigarette, Velma said, "I'll finish this while you're getting undressed."

Apple came out of his dream about sitting tall in the saddle on a giant of a white horse. He opened his eyes. He was looking at a ceiling.

His anxiety at this passed swiftly. He had recalled where he was and why. Scoffing at the plaster above, he settled to enjoying his embrace of Velma Wilde, who was asleep with her head on his chest. A reliving of their languid love-making he would enjoy later.

This state of affairs might have continued had it not been that Apple, his mind nicely unjumbled, began to worry about the snooping he ought to be doing on the estate.

It had to be got underway as soon as possible, he thought. A footprint, for instance, could be erased by animals or the weather. There would be time later for more dalliance with the delightful and sensuous Velma. The caper came first.

Denying to himself that his decision to act at once was related either to the ceiling or the growing numbness of his right arm, on which Velma was lying, Apple started on careful extrication. He managed it without waking Velma, whom he then tucked in cozily.

Apple didn't hurry over the task of getting into his clothes, which lay in a scatter. That it was three o'clock in the afternoon rather than in the morning he found piquant. He mused on what a rogue he was, to be sure.

Swinging his arm to help the circulation, Apple left the room and went downstairs. He vetoed immediately the idea of stopping by to get Monico. When he only had himself to worry about, he was braver.

The guest-house lay in a mid-afternoon torpor. The desk was deserted, the bar doing poor business, the chintz seating mostly empty. Those present were reading or dozing. Apple sauntered out the front way.

Within minutes he was parking his van in exactly the same place as last night. Mist still hid it from the road, he noted on walking back there. He crossed to the wall, climbed it and set off over the rough ground.

Reasonably confident of being on the same route, although not following a path, Apple went at an easy walking pace. He watched the ground ahead. Daylight helping to fight the mist, visibility was a good ten yards.

Soon Apple judged himself to be getting near to the region of chuckles and clicks. He bent closer to the ground. That he didn't find anything straight away was only to be expected. When he still hadn't seen anything after passing through the glade and coming back to it again, he was disappointed.

Apple also felt cheated. His emotions reasoned that as a man who had forsaken a willing wench and a warm bed for this, he deserved far better. It wasn't fair.

Apple was reminding himself that he could be back there fast, maybe without Velma even knowing of his absence, when his nose caught a new odour. He took a deep sniff.

Fried bacon? he mused. Or was it ham? Perhaps with a bit of kidney?

Making a half-turn, Apple began to move in the direction of what seemed to be the odour's source. He sniffed persistently as he went. Fried bacon or ham became a butcher's shop. That became a slaughterhouse.

The odour continued to grow less pleasant as Apple walked

and sniffed, until, served by a breeze coming this way, it suddenly turned into a stink.

At which point Apple realised that he had, of course, come up behind that pigpen near the gate. If he were any closer, he would be getting the full blast.

Apple's next realisation was of an inner turmoil. His sense of hearing was trying to elbow aside his sense of smell. With no reluctance, he let it.

Faintly, there was a clicking sound. It seemed to be close at hand and coming from somewhere behind him. That it was getting louder was absolute.

Apple looked around quickly for somewhere to hide. There were several convenient rocks. He chose and ran to the tallest. It would have been fine for Mr. Average but it fitted Apple like a shrunken head.

He crouched behind the rock uncomfortably, his chin on a kneecap. Keeping stone still, warning himself not to allow this to make him neurotic about ambushes, he listened to the sounds of approach.

A figure gradually appeared through the mist. It took shape as a man. He was dead ahead, and Apple waited for him to look up. In any case, he was turning to come right this way.

Apple noted details. Middle-aged man in tweed cap and a tweed overcoat. Thin face with bags under sharp eyes. Could be anything from veterinarian to village schoolteacher. Carries a lunch-pail; occasionally, its handle clicks.

And of course, Apple thought, occasionally the old-timer chuckles at his own jokes.

Now, for the second time since appearing, the tweedy man made an abrupt turn. This new change of direction took him out of view. To keep him in sight, Apple was obliged to edge squattily around his rock.

He went on doing that until the man, after making two more acute turnings, began to fade into the mist. Apple got up.

His height afforded him a good scan of where the man had walked. There were no paths.

Apple followed. He kept just within sight of the one he had nicknamed Tweedy, who continued to change direction every few yards, and who obliged presently by chuckling.

Meanwhile, the smell of the pigpen was growing stronger. When it had become so unpleasant that Apple began to breathe through his mouth, its source appeared.

The man went straight to a dilapidated gate in the wall of the extensive pigpen. Beyond, the pink beasts lolled in mud or stood shoulder-deep in murky puddles.

After footing the gate closed behind him, Tweedy went on. He moved around two puddles but then stepped directly into a third.

Apple, watching and following, twitched with surprise. But, unexpectedly, the man did not sink in up to the knee. His sturdy boot got only its sole covered with water.

That went on happening as he made his way across the animal pen, stepping with some deliberation from pool to pool. Almost, he seemed to be walking on the surface of the water. Aided by the mist, it was an eerie sight.

In the centre of the pigpen stood a rough, stunted structure: three drystone walls no more than a yard high; they were covered with a piece of corrugated tin that was held down with rocks; a sack covered the opening.

Holding his nose against the atrocious stench, Apple came to a stop beside a tree. He watched Tweedy go to the central structure, bend, push aside the sacking, go inside and out of sight; watched and told himself: The laboratory, of course. The secret lab which, cleverly, had been hidden by being out here in full view. And guarded with great efficiency by a stink —one that probably had help from chemicals in being awful. Any human type of guard would, obviously, give the game away.

Again cleverly, Apple thought on in admiration, staff came only at night or in suitable covering weather, such as today's. They came by countryside, not road, and always walked in a zigzag fashion to avoid creating a path. The pigpen's muck they crossed on solid cement patches which were automatically maintained slightly covered with water. The plan was altogether brilliant.

And brilliant was the light that Apple saw a split second after he felt the fierce pain in the back of his head, and before everything vanished, himself included.

Returning to consciousness, Apple flickered his eyes open. What he saw first was the roof of a cavern. Smooth, without stalactites, it vaulted grandly to a height of thirty feet.

Assuring himself that a cavern roof definitely could not be classed as a ceiling, Apple started to sense out the rest of the situation.

He was lying on the floor, on sacks. His hands were tied behind, his feet were bound at the ankles. The pigpen stink was faint, but decidedly present. The pain in the back of his skull was bearable: the blow had been delivered by someone who knew about such things. Lighting was supplied by electric lamps set high on the rough walls.

With difficulty Apple sat up. He looked around at the scene at ground level. It would have been no disappointment to a Frankenstein.

About the size of a tennis court, the place was scattered with work-benches and tables. These bore every kind of glass or metal apparatus from simple retorts to the complex indescribable. Along one curving wall stood immense copper vats. Elsewhere there were two large, open bowls from which vapour rose lazily. In several places there were piles of crates. By the nearest wall a spiral staircase of wrought iron climbed to an opening the size of a squat doorway. And that, Apple thought, leads to the pigpen's centre structure.

Survey concluded, he considered the situation in respect of himself. It was tricky.

As he had been sapped and captured, Apple thought, the laboratory's security people must have assumed him to be more than merely a busybody. Perhaps they had assumed him to be no less than Clever Freddy.

Perhaps, no, Apple amended: certainly. They would have had an eye on all the possibles among the film people, including dog-handler Tim Gordon. Catching him here on the snoop, they had naturally enough jumped to the Clever Freddy indentification.

Therefore, Apple realised, there was only one thing he could do to get himself out of this. He would have to blow his cover. But not, of course, to the rank and file. He would talk only to the head man, who would know how to check with Upstairs, and who would keep the truth under his head man's hat.

Apple shouted, "Hey!"

Before the word had stopped echoing around the cavern, a male voice with a Scottish accent said, "Aye, thon long streak of misery's awake."

A similar voice said, "Not before time."

"And I only gave him a wee tap."

"You and your taps. Come on."

Into view from around the closest pile of crates walked two men. The first was Tweedy, still in his coat and cap but minus the lunch-pail. The second man was half his age and twice his size, with an aspect that immediately caused Apple to christen him Goon.

The big man, crew-cut to rug length, had a boxer's features and small eyes of blank blue. Suitably, he wore the kind of turtle-neck sweater that cartoonists always put on their bullies.

Even if he hadn't been carrying a shotgun, he would still have looked a menace, if only because of those blank blue eyes.

The two men came to a stop nearby. Looking down grimly at Apple, Tweedy asked, "You properly awake now?"

Coldly: "That should be quite evident."

"And ready for a few questions?"

"Sorry to be a disappointment to you," Apple said. "I talk only to the top man around here. I want to see him at once." He added, "Please."

The older man said, "I'm going to disappoint you as well, mister. See, you'll have to make do with me. So start thinking about a few answers."

"No, thank you."

"You're in no position to say that. You've been caught snooping around."

"I insist on seeing the principal."

"You were snooping near here last night, too," Tweedy said. He gave his chuckle—and Apple realised that it wasn't a laugh but a type of cough. "Right?"

"I'm saying nothing."

"Which means yes. In any case, I heard you. I heard those great strides of yours."

The other man finally spoke. With an amiable nod, Goon said, "He's a long streak of misery right enough."

"All this is wasting time," Apple said. "However, I will tell you this much: I am not an enemy."

"Says you."

"Says me. So before anything else, would you be kind enough to untie me. The circulation's not getting to my hands and feet."

The older man looked mildly sympathetic. "If I did, you might try something."

"When I'm being covered by a shotgun? No, thanks. You've been watching too much television."

"I'll loose your hands," Tweedy said, coming forward. "Your big feet will have to stay as they are." Quickly, he untied the cord on the wrists and returned to his place.

"That's better," Apple said. "Thank you." He massaged the red marks on his skin. They were as superficial as the blockage on his circulation, but he had at least succeeded in getting his hands free. Feeling less insecure, he raised his voice for an authoritative, "Now let's talk about me seeing the man in control here, shall we, gentlemen?"

Swaying his shoulders in exasperation, Tweedy said, "Why do you keep on and on about a top man? Mister, *you've* been watching too much television."

"What the hell d'you mean?"

"You must think there's a master criminal lurking in the bloody shadows."

Apple frowned. "Who's talking about criminals?"

"Listen," Tweedy said levelly. "You know what we are. So we want to know what you are and what your game is. Then we want to know what to do with you."

Goon turned to his companion. The earnest, childlike way he spoke lent icy veracity to his flat "Well, we could always shoot him."

Apple opened his mouth slowly as he looked from one man to the other. He began to suspect that all was not what he thought. He said, "Now wait a minute."

Tweedy, oddly courteous: "Yes?"

"If you think I'm Clever Freddy, you're wrong."

It was the turn of the two men to do some examining of faces, each other's and their prisoner's. This told Apple that they had never heard of the name. His suspicion grown fatter, he nevertheless said, "You must take me to your head man immediately."

Goon said, "I know a neat joke about a Martian that lands his flying saucer and says to this man—"

"Shut your blather," Tweedy snapped. "You must've been into the product."

"Only a wee dram," Goon said, blinking defensively. "Not enough to wet a flea."

"If you don't watch your step, I'll be having a word with your father. You hear?"

Goon grumbled, "I hear ye."

Apple, who had been having another look around at the equipment, particularly the copper vats, thought he began to see the truth of it.

He asked, "This isn't a laboratory?"

Again the men looked at him as though he were talking some unknown language. They understood perfectly, however, his next question. It related to the Cavalry Stampede.

"That was neat, all right," Goon said, smiling proudly. "I did very well there."

The older man admitted, "Aye, you didn't do too badly."

Apple asked, "And who pushed that man off the rock?"

Goon, grinning: "Me, with a long stick."

"And how about the wind machine?"

"Ah, now that took me a bit longer to set up."

Apple was going to ask next about the old man who had talked jinx at the guest-house, but Tweedy said, "This isn't getting us anywhere. No more questions."

"Okay, then let me give you a few answers," Apple said. "My name, as you must know because you must have checked my pockets for papers, is Tim Gordon. I'm a dog-handler with the film company, which you also probably know. I was watching today out of curiosity bred of boredom. I'm not the least bit interested in what you people're up to down here."

The older man asked with faint grandness, "Then how d'you know we're up to anything?"

Apple spread his arms. "If this isn't an illicit whisky still, I'm a Dutch cigar."

"Illegal, mister, not illicit," Tweedy said. "We think it's perfectly licit."

"Whatever you want to think is fine with me," Apple said. "And congratulations, by the way, on your camouflage. It's brilliant. I mean that sincerely."

"Don't waste your time with flattery, mister. You're in trouble. You don't seem to realise that."

"You're right, I don't. Why should I be in trouble?"

"Because we can't just let you go wandering off. You know too much and no doubt you would talk about it."

"No, I wouldn't."

Ignoring him, the older man went on, "You could destroy a nice wee operation—not to mention the law trouble we'd be in. So you see, mister, we have to do something with you."

Apple, worried, blustered, "You can't keep me down here indefinitely."

"Oh?" Tweedy said. He said it slowly and with his head on one side. He seemed to be considering the idea.

Apple felt chilled. From the stampeded horses and the wind machine incident, either of which could have caused death or severe injury, he knew that the bootleggers were ruthless. Certainly, Goon was prepared to play any vicious game.

Apple offered no resistance when now the older man ordered him to hand over his car keys, only asking, as he tossed them across, "Why?"

"So I can move it from this immediate region, naturally. We don't want to leave a trail, do we? No, we don't. Where did you park it, mister?"

"I really have no idea. I climbed the wall to ramble, and got lost. That's why I'm here."

But Tweedy had stopped listening. He turned to Goon with, "It'll be somewhere nearby. I'll take it and go to see the others. We'll decide what to do about him."

"Shouldn't be much problem about that."

"Make sure he doesn't get away."

The big man said warmly, "Right you are."

Tweedy turned and moved off. "See you later."

"Hey, wait a minute," Apple said. He pushed with his hands to get to his feet. Being bound at the ankles, he was thrown off balance. He fell down again sideways.

By the time Apple got himself back into a sit, the older man had climbed the spiral staircase. He passed out of view through the doorway. The cavern's silence was rippled by a faint splashing sound from outside.

Goon cleared his throat boredly, as if he had realised that this wasn't going to be any fun. He was standing two yards away, feet spread, mildly attentive. The double-barrelled shotgun he held down at arms' length and with his finger near the trigger.

Apple mused: If I can't get the better of this character in the thinking department, I deserve whatever happens to me. But Apple mused thus to give himself confidence. He knew very well that it wasn't always easy to outwit the dim-witted.

Goon asked, "What you thinking about, mister?"

"I?" Apple said, as though cogitation was something he never went in for. "Not a single thing."

"Except that I ought to be a push-over on account of I'm a bit on the slow side. Eh?"

Letting that go by, Apple decided to stick to Training Four's advice for the prisoner-and-gunman situation. You had to build up to the attack slowly by lulling the enemy into a sense of security. The best way to do that was with easy-mannered talk. And the best kind of talk was about the talker himself. He was giving.

Apple said, "You and your friend are mistaken about me." He smiled in forgiveness.

"How do you mean?" the big man asked.

"I wouldn't dream of telling a soul about this place. I'm not the type."

"What would the type be?"

"Well, I'm not sure."

"I've often wondered," Goon said dully, sighing.

Apple went on with talk about his Tim Gordon persona. He mentioned his love of dogs (Goon said he was a cat man himself), dropped casually that his mother was a Scot (Goon said his was English), confessed to his dislike of being so tall (Goon said that was no way to talk), and lavished praise on the beauty of the Highlands (Goon said give him Glasgow any day).

Apple told himself not to be discouraged. Not sure of how much time he had, he passed on to phase two. Which was to try to get the gunman to come within reach.

"Anyway," Apple said cozily, "when that nice friend of yours returns, I'm sure we'll be able to arrive at an amiable understanding." He patted his pockets. "You don't happen to have a cigarette, do you?"

"As a matter of fact," the big man said, "I have several."

"Oh. Well, good."

"Would you like one?"

"Yes, please."

Apple hadn't expected it to work. He had tried the ploy as a matter of form—almost, it could be said, of tradition. Therefore he was taken by surprise when Goon, producing a pack of cigarettes, came over at once to stand well within touching distance. Apple had nothing planned.

"There," the big man said, tossing the packet down. "Help yourself. But only one, mind."

Apple's hands were as slow in getting out a cigarette as his mind was busy in trying to produce a plan for instant action. Punch upward? Grab the legs? Go for the Achilles tendons? Bash head to knee?

And then it was too late. After plucking back his packet of cigarettes, Goon moved in reverse to where he had been before.

Depressed, Apple said, "Thank you."

"That's all right."

Recovering: "But I don't have any matches."

Goon put his pack in one pocket as from another he brought out a lighter. He tossed it across. "Catch."

Apple did. With the cigarette in his mouth, he started to act fumbles on the lighter's top. "I can never get these bloody things to work."

"There's a knack to it," the big man said, coming over. He sank to a one-leg kneel immediately in front of Apple. The shotgun was pointed aside. Goon took the lighter and thumbed it into flame.

Tense, Apple told himself while puffing at the cigarette that this was the moment. All he had to do was push Goon off balance and grab the gun.

Due to his tenseness, plus his mind being elsewhere, Apple's throat wasn't prepared for the passage of smoke. It contracted. Apple rounded his shoulders as he went into a spasm of wheezing.

It was a long one. His face turned dusky pink and his eyes watered. When, panting himself to recovery, he wiped dry his vision, he saw that Goon had gone back to his original standing position.

They looked at each other like old and tedious friends. After a moment the big man asked, "Do you get 'em often, those attacks?"

Apple shook his head. Next, he nodded. "Whenever I sit on damp floors. D'you think I could have a chair?"

"No," Goon said. "You're safer down there."

Affably: "Whatever you say. This is fine with me. I'm very easy to get along with."

"Don't burn your fingers."

Apple puffed at his cigarette fervently. The time element had him worried. He could imagine Tweedy on his way back here at this moment. With a bunch of hard-eyed, ruthless bootleggers. Even if they didn't kill him, or do him any physical damage, they could easily decide to keep him a prisoner for as long as it suited them. That wouldn't be funny.

Apple asked, "What was that joke you said you knew, about a Martian?"

Brightening, Goon said, "It's about a Martian."

"Really?"

"I'll tell it to you, if you like."

Apple gestured. "Please do. Feel free."

With a lurking smile, the big man told his joke. Following delivery of the punch line (which Apple didn't understand), he surged into laughter. It was of the near-helpless variety. He sagged at the knees, bowed his back, lolled his head. He was in a twaddle of delight.

Straightening at length, he sighed, wiped his eyes with a sweater cuff and said, "Och, it does you good, a wee chortle."

Apple, who had acted a laugh until his cheeks ached, agreed with fervour. That was not acted. He knew he had found the chink in his guard's armour. All he need do to create the safe opportunity for jumping Goon was get him to laugh.

Grinning both for himself and for show, Apple put his cigarette out while asking, "Did you ever hear the one about the actress and the bishop?"

Strongly, for emphasis, the big man shook his head. "No, I never did. Go on."

"Right," Apple said, trying to remember the joke. "It goes like this."

"Yes? Yes?"

Apple couldn't remember. His grin sank to a flat slit. He could recall no detail of the joke, though he kept promoting it with "Wait'll you hear this one," and "It's hilarious." He finally had nothing to say at all, except "Sorry, I can't seem to bring it to mind."

The big man had subsided to glumness, after which his eyes had changed their expression from dull reproof to forced suspicion. He said, "Maybe you never did know a joke about an actress and a bishop."

"Yes, I did. I do."

"So how come you can't remember it?"

"Because of sitting on . . ." Apple began, and then, because he had already tried that one, switched his excuse from floor to feet: "Sitting with my ankles tied."

"What's that got to do with it?"

"The restricted circulation. It causes pain and numbness. They interfere with my thinking."

"Oh, all right," Goon said, swaying in hope and surrender. "You can take the cord off."

Holding up his hands, Apple flexed the fingers stiffly. "Can't. My hands're still numb." As the chances of making Goon laugh looked slim, he had decided on another attempt at the drawn-captor gambit. "You'll have to do it."

Sighing like an abused stepfather, the big man came across. He knelt as before; but this time, before tackling the knot with both hands, he rested his shotgun at an upright slant against Apple's bent legs.

Apple went weak all over. There was only one thing worse than staring into the barrel of a gun at close range, as far as his emotions were concerned, and that was staring into two barrels. He could not have moved a fraction for the gift of ten Clever Freddys.

Tossing the untied cord aside, the big man got up with his shotgun and went backwards to his place. "Right," he said. "Now let's have that joke."

Apple nodded. He continued doing so while he warmed up

again from the coolness of dread. It was as if he was agreeing with himself that there was even less hope now of his remembering that joke or any other.

He said feebly, "We'll have to wait for a while until the circulation gets going."

Goon looked away from him with tired aggravation. After sending the look on a tour of the cavern he brought it back with, "Oh, all right. I'll tell you one while we're waiting. But yours better be good."

"It's hilarious."

"Well, there were these three typists, see," the big man started. Instantly, he produced a smiling, confidential manner. It flourished as he went on with his narrative build-up.

Soon Apple recognised the joke. He had heard it dozens of times. He interrupted with "Excuse me."

"What?"

"I know that one."

Goon made another instant switch—to glowering menace. "Oh, you do, do you?"

Quickly realising his mistake in trying to do the right thing, Apple asked lyingly, "It's where they all buy the same kind of dress, isn't it?"

Relieved and scornful, the big man wagged his head. "Not at all. It's nothing like that. Listen." He returned to his narrative, smiling again.

Apple began to prepare himself for action. As though in eagerness to hear the joke with perfect clarity, he edged forward until his buttocks were close to his heels and his chest was nearing his knees.

Going into the final stretch, Goon started to splutter. He managed to hold on until the punch line, which came out as an unintelligible gasp, then threw himself gratefully into his wiggle-wobble laugh.

Apple didn't wait any longer. Pushing off with both hands,

he jack-knifed up from his folded crouch. Up and forward. He leapt to the big man, who was unaware of the approach, slapped at the gun and used his shoulder to send Goon staggering.

The shotgun fell. Apple, stalking fast and tall, went after the shocked man and caught him with a comfortingly correct judo chop to the side of the neck. His eyes turning up, Goon sank heavily to the floor. He was out.

Apple ran to the spiral staircase.

Cautiously, he pushed aside the curtain of sacking. The only animate entities around were pigs. Caution gladly discarded, Apple stepped outside into the stink and straightened up from his stoop.

He looked down at the ground. Away in every direction stretched an array of puddles, some small, some like baby lakes. They all looked deep. Apple chose the nearest, testing with the toe of his shoe.

It met solidity after half an inch of water. Apple flattened his whole foot, and, taking a chance, stepped flatly into the next puddle. He had no time to waste: Goon could already be recovering, Tweedy could be on his way back with colleagues and dire intentions.

Apple stayed lucky. Until the fifth step. With that, he went half-way up his shin into the slush. Somehow he wasn't the least bit surprised.

But he was startled, for the sudden drop threw his upper body forward. It seemed that he was bound to fall headlong into a large pool of slimy water. He wheeled his arms madly, jerked his trunk to and fro, moaned.

It did no good. A fall was inevitable—unless, he saw, he steadied himself by bringing his other leg down into the sludge. Which is what he did. It worked.

Ignoring an attack of self-pity, just as he was keeping his

mind off the stench and his immersed lower legs, Apple bent from the waist for a closer look at the puddles. Some, he saw, had edgings that were solid: cement, not mud.

From there on it was simple. Stepping out of the pool, Apple went on his way without further mishap by choosing those puddles which had the now-recognizable signs.

The only drawback was that, in keeping in a stoop in order to see clearly, he had his nose closer to the awesome stink. He bore it well.

At the gate Apple straightened. Passing through, he began to run. He did so in vast relief: at getting away from the smell, and at leaving half the danger behind.

Urgency still surged strongly in Apple, especially with regard to Goon, whom, he told himself, he had been lucky to outwit; obviously, the big man was not the cretin he appeared to be. Apple knew he should have spared the time needed to hide or disable the double-barrelled shotgun.

Now, at late afternoon, the mist was as strong as ever. There was nothing to be seen but trees and rocks. There was nothing to be heard but the thud-squeak of wet footfalls.

Apple ran on at full pelt. Although the stink's main force had slackened off, there was still a powerful odour rising from immediately below, where sopping trouser legs flapped against chill flesh.

Reaching the boundary wall, Apple climbed over onto the road. The odour was worse when he wasn't running. About to set off again, he froze at the sound of an approaching car. But it was coming from behind, and he reckoned that the Tweedy and Co. danger would be coming from the direction of town.

Nevertheless, Apple stayed close to the wall, and ready to leap it, until the car pierced the mist. It was driven by an older woman. She passed without once taking her determined gaze off the road.

Apple went back to his run. He didn't spare himself, and

not only on account of the stink and the danger. A codicil to his urgency was the fact that unless he did something quickly about his squelching feet, he would be sure to come down with a cold.

That thought gave Apple a stronger response of concern than the one given by his major urgency. It was so mundane.

Presently, he drew level with the place where he had parked his van. He was back on the road again in one minute after a detour to check that, as expected, Tweedy had helped himself to the Austin.

Another vehicle came along from behind, sound first. Apple left his stand by the wall when he saw a milk truck. He stuck out his thumb. The driver waved regretfully at his no-riders placard.

Running on, Apple wondered about the long-term situation. What was he going to do to protect himself from the gang of bootleggers? Were they likely to come searching for him at the guest-house?

Apple didn't know the answer to either question, and now there were motor sounds from ahead. He was fast in getting to and climbing the wall. His return climb was slower, tired, when the glimpsed non-enemy car had passed.

However, Apple forced his wearying legs into maintaining a steady run. Even though he had grown more confident of being able to evade danger for the moment, from either direction, there were still his feet to consider. Alas.

Two more cars went by in the direction of town/guest-house before Apple got a reaction to his thumb.

The large grey Bentley, driven by a woman in headscarf and sun-glasses, the sole rider, came to a stop a little way ahead. Apple ran on, opened the front passenger door and let out music.

"Oh," he said, pausing. "It's you."

Helen Parker had taken off her sun-glasses. She now

reached leisurely to the dashboard and pressed a button. The tape of vintage jazz fell silent.

"Yes, it is," the supporting actress said in her quiet, mellifluous voice with the precise diction. Her features were as calm, and as attractive, as usual.

That changed quickly. Her eyes widened, her nostrils shrank small, her hairline went up under the scarf, her mouth opened. She could have been auditioning for a horror movie.

"Jesus Christ," she whispered.

Apple said with a cringe, "Yes, I know. It's an awful smell. Sorry about that. I stepped in . . . um . . . one of those bogs. You know. The stinking kind."

"That wasn't terribly bright of you."

"Agreed. I'm sopping wet."

Helen Parker blew out heavily and put her sun-glasses back on. She said, "Get in, please."

"You mean it? Really?"

"Of course I mean it, Tim. Do get in."

"That's very decent of you," Apple said, crouching his way inside. "Under the circumstances." He closed the door.

The actress shrugged. "I was raised on a farm. I dare say I can stand a bit of ripe atmosphere. A bog, did you say?"

Apple nodded absently. He was both admiring Helen Parker's khaki safari suit and realising that she had just used his supposed first name.

The Bentley whooshed away. With equal ease the pigpen smell rose in the confined space and persisted even after the driver, pressing buttons, had lowered all the windows.

Not daring to look at Helen Parker, Apple worked at diversion by talking. He was trying to keep himself from being embarrassed as well as hoping to lessen the stink's impact.

Apple talked to the mist about the world of acting, stage as opposed to film. He hoped he made sense: for one thing, he had meagre knowledge of the subject, and for another, part of his mind was busy recalling segments of that joke about the actress and the bishop.

Meanwhile, a car appearing ahead and coming this way, Apple sank down in the seat until his head was level with his knees. It was also closer to his lower legs. Had he been alone, he would have whimpered.

The car having passed, Apple, despite the stench, rose only slightly from his hiding slouch, merely enough to enable him to see through the bottom of the windshield. He went on talking and not mentioning bishops.

When the guest-house took shape out of the mist, Apple was glad. He said, "There's Blancairn."

"Yes, it's a pretty place," Helen Parker said. Pressing a button to bring the jazz back to life, she drove straight on past the house.

There was no talking on the rest of the drive. Nor, on Apple's part, was there much thinking. Soothed with the spirit of a bygone New Orleans but assaulted by an atrocious smell, his body comfortably at rest but his neck craning up, he found it difficult to relate either to the incident he had experienced in the illegal still or to the one he was presently undergoing.

Apple stayed in his low slump until the Bentley began to slow in the town's centre. Sitting up cautiously, the first thing he noticed was his Austin van. It was neatly parked in the square.

Helen Parker stopped opposite the hotel. "Come along," she said, opening her door. She made a fast, air-gulping exit. Apple did the same. He went around towards the supporting actress, who said, "I think I'll leave the windows down for the time being."

"Good idea," Apple toadied. "It's not likely there'd be car thieves in this part of the world."

"But there're joy-riders. Kids, I suppose. They took the

script girl's old Jag for a couple of hours and scratched up the front. However . . ." She turned away.

At a distance of several feet Apple followed, into the hotel lobby, across it and into a lift. He was aware of stares, sniffs and the squelching of his shoes. That the lift was empty came as a relief. The trip was over before the stench had time to spread itself.

On the top floor they went into a suite that was identical to Arthur Reed's. They didn't halt at once. Elegant sitting-room led to exquisite bedroom, which led to sumptuous, carpeted star-type bathroom.

Turning on taps at the tub, Helen Parker said, "A hot soak is what you need, Tim."

"Yes," Apple said, thinking, There's that name again.

"Throw your wet things outside. I'll send them down for cleaning and drying." She went out and left the door ajar.

Now not thinking a single thing, Apple stripped naked. His shoes and socks he wrapped in his trousers. He crouched shyly to set this bundle through the door opening as well as to go over to the bath.

Minutes later, when he was lying back in the deep water, Helen Parker came in. Apple started to stand up. Catching himself in time, he splashed low again and resisted the urge to cross his arms on his chest.

But Apple was unable to prevent a cringe of shock when, after lowering the lavatory seat-cover, the supporting actress sat down on it.

Crossing her legs comfortably, Helen Parker said, "You know, Tim, you fascinate me."

Apple stared. "I do?"

"You do. You're a very rare bird. I'd like to know what makes you tick."

Not sure if this was a safe direction for the conversation to take, Apple began to soap himself. "Actually," he said, "I'm merely a dog-handler."

The actress shook her head emphatically. "There's more to you than that."

"Well, yes, as a matter of fact there is. I do have a strong feeling for music. Any kind. But I'll tell you something."

"Yes, Tim?"

"I can't play a musical instrument."

Helen Parker nodded with eyes shrewd. "Declines to be considered more than the apparent. The modesty syndrome."

"I beg your pardon?"

"This is fascinating. The search for the real tick-maker. And music isn't it. Tell me more about yourself, Tim."

Boldly soaping an armpit, Apple said, "Well, there's literature. Books are very important to me."

The actress asked, "What's your favourite reading?"

Truthfully, still bold: "Spy novels."

"That's significant."

"Is it?"

"The cloak, the mask, the pretence."

Apple asked, "Did you ever read *The Mask of Eric?*"

Helen Parker shook her head. "Sad to say, I have no time to read anything but scripts."

"Naturally, every producer's after you, Miss Parker."

"Call me Hellie, Tim. We've got to get to know each other a lot better."

"Of course, Hellie," Apple said. "Certainly."

"And yes, it's true that I'm besieged by producers," the actress said airily. She went on to tell of what a draw she was at the box office.

Apple might have dwelled more on how uncharacteristic it seemed of her to talk this way if he hadn't been so busy with self-congratulation: he had changed the subject from Tim Gordon.

After a minute, however, Helen Parker said, "Anyway, let's get back to you. Let's see if I can peek behind the mask."

"Eric's mask, in that book, is made of gold. It's an antique. And a Russian spy steals it."

"Good," the actress said. She got up. "How about some food? I'm starving. I could have them send up something tasty. Does that sound interesting?"

"Wonderful," Apple said. "But you've reminded me of my dog." He explained about room-bound Monico.

Helen Parker went out on, "Fine. I'll take care of that matter as well."

While continuing dazedly with his bath, Apple wondered if he were hallucinating; listened to the actress call down to order hot turkey sandwiches and tea; heard her telephone the guest-house to arrange for Monico's food and outdoor visit; worked at getting *The Mask of Eric*'s plot in sequence so that he could tell it smoothly.

When Helen Parker returned, she was in a robe. There were no signs of her safari suit. "All set," she said. "And your dried things will be sent up with the food."

"Fast service."

"But there's no hurry about the clothes, is there?"

"None at all, Hellie," Apple said. He was beginning to believe all this and get in the mood of it. Now, on hearing the actress ask if he wanted her to soap his back, he merely said, "Sure." After all, he argued inside, why shouldn't she like him for his own true self?

That question put Apple back in wonderland for a while, during which time Helen Parker, sitting on the bath edge, soaped and rinsed his shoulders with a sponge. He still hadn't returned to full belief when he was told by Helen as she rose, "You've had long enough, Tim. It's my turn now. Up you get." After reaching for a towel, which she held spreadingly ready, she stood watching and waiting like a mum.

Was that the answer? Apple queried, adding disappointment to his threatening embarrassment. Did she, because of being two or three years older than himself, look upon him as a child?

Helen Parker, giving the towel a matador shake, said in bland complacency, "Come along, Tim."

What Apple saw throughout his fast and furtive, saggy and sidewaysy exit from the bath was a market-place in India. The vision worked. He was able to see reality again, blushless, once safely standing close to the supporting actress and taking over the towel.

At which point the situation made a turn that settled, quite decisively, the questions relating to mums and possible hallucinations.

Smiling faintly but with a hint of lewdness, Helen Parker reached up her arms and put what part of them she could around Apple's neck. She drew his head down.

They began to kiss.

Apple released his hold on the towel, which fell. Next, with no separation of mouths, the actress shuffled out of her robe, which fell also. She was naked. That nudity she pressed against Apple's wetness. He didn't draw back.

They went into a roving, slippery embrace, one which, matched by the kiss, grew quickly more passionate.

They sank to the thick carpet. Their embrace became half-value as they each put one hand to use for caressing. Apple was having a wonderful, astounded time of it. He wasn't at all surprised when the doorbell chimed. An interruption seemed inevitable.

Against active, experienced lips he mumbled, "Someone's at the door."

"I know. It'll be the food."

"We should answer."

"I suppose so," the actress murmured, the words blurred. "But maybe they'll go away."

"That's true."

The kiss went creatively on. The chime sounded again.

"Ah well," Helen Parker said, clearly, easing her lips free. "We'll be more comfortable on the bed anyway."

"That's a splendid idea."

"If you'd like to see to the food?"

Apple got up. With the towel wrapped around his lower body he passed through bedroom to sitting-room. He opened wide the suite door.

Outside, a man in a white jacket stood behind a service trolley. On its top were dishes, on its bottom shelf footwear and clothes. The man was Rex, the fair-haired operative.

He stiffened. He stared. He creaked upright slowly from his pushing position on the trolley.

"Yes, fine," Apple said briskly, his spirits soaring. "Bring it in and leave it over there, mm? Thank you." Turning, he sauntered back to the bedroom doorway.

During those scant seconds, Appleton Porter learned the meaning of true happiness.

It was dark when he left the hotel. He felt buoyant; felt as he imagined he would if he were famous; felt, strangely, not as tall as he ought to be.

Even so, Apple forced his mind to the mundane on reaching his van. Not touching it to begin with, he used his cigarette lighter for illumination in making all the standard body and chassis checks for a booby-trap. Next, he lifted the hood to look at the motor.

Apple was not being melodramatic, playing the spy game. The illegal whisky still's elaborate camouflage showed that bootlegging was a lucrative venture, one well worth protecting.

The Austin seemed clean, and nothing happened when Apple tried the door handle (unlocked), got in carefully, searched for the ignition keys in all the usual hiding places (empty), and started the motor by crossing wires.

Still alert and taut of nerve, Apple drove off. Once out of town, however, with nothing visible in his rear-view mirror, he relaxed a little and allowed himself the pleasure of dwelling on his evening with Helen Parker.

From the love-making to the good strong tea, everything had been wonderful, Apple allowed. Furthermore, Hellie had appeared to enjoy his recounting of the plot of *The Mask of Eric*. Their parting had been sophisticatedly casual: they would see each other around.

That the incident shouldn't be in the public domain had been established neatly by Helen Parker saying "You're not, I'm sure, a kiss-and-teller."

Until he came to the guest-house, where he parked and went inside, Apple enjoyed recalling the sensuality, as well as feeling a cad on account of Velma, plus reminding himself of his exceptional virility.

At Blancairn most people were still at dinner. Apple slipped upstairs and got his dog (who greeted him coolly), came down again and went back outside. There was enough light from the windows for him to walk Monico around the house—and to notice at last that the mist was fading.

As he walked, Apple gave his mind to the situation with the bootleggers, meaning: how was he going to protect himself?

First, by doing the citizenly proper thing—reporting the still to the authorities—he could have the gang taken out of circulation. He needn't become involved personally; an anonymous telephone call would do the trick.

Trouble was, though, Apple mused, the police might not be able to round them all up. It could even be one of those rural conspiracies, with half the county's families involved. Those remaining free may seek a bloody revenge on the fink.

On guard as he walked as to what might be hidden in the darkness, Apple considered the second possibility. If he could contact the bootleggers without endangering himself, he could repeat what he had said before, that he had no intentions of giving them away. That had a chance of working, being more believable now that he wasn't under a gun. If he was able to make contact.

Possibility three, Apple thought without enthusiasm, was to do absolutely nothing—except stay on the alert, and worry.

He was more enthusiastic about one final possibility. At least on a personal level. Professionally, it could be a total disaster. His body would be safer but the mission would be endangered if there were dozens of policemen all around the location, as well as Blancairn and the other film-folk lodgings.

This horde of official bodyguards could be arranged for simply with a telephone call, one made to the authorities as, supposedly, a spokesman for the Scottish Nationalist Independent Freedom Fighters. This underground group was first cousin to the Irish Republican Army. He would say that unless local filming ended at once on *My Candle Burns,* which absurdity was an insult to the Scots bard, SNIFF would take violent action to bring about that cessation. With the separatist group being infamous for its bombings and other terrorist activities, the police wouldn't dare ignore such a call.

Apple was in the midst of declining to acknowledge that there did exist another possibility—give up and go home—when he went around a corner and met the new gardener.

They stopped. McKay said, "Aye, I did hear as you'd found the wee dog."

"Him being taken was a practical joke," Apple said. "But I don't think it's so funny." He explained about the map and the cave.

Smiling, the gardener shook his head. "You fillum people is rare 'uns."

On a beforethought, Apple asked, "What would you have done if we'd all left? You might have lost your job."

"Och, I'm only temporary here anyway. I can always get a bit of farm work. It takes no skill to dig ditches and feed animals, y'know."

"Right," Apple said, pleased. "Good night." He walked on quickly in case he thanked McKay for his idea.

Circling the house again, Apple got in his van—after Monico, who took the passenger seat, and who didn't seem to mind having the safety-belt fastened across him.

Thus reminded of the hit-and-push incident, Apple wished he had known about the script girl's Jaguar earlier, though it would have had to be right after the theft to be useful. He could have dusted the car for latent prints, then tried for a match with his suspects. And getting their fingerprints would have been an interesting venture. By now, of course, usage would have obliterated any spoor left by Clever Freddy.

Instead of blaming himself for not being more diligent—searching for the big chase car—Apple took consolation in feeling convinced that the wily free lance spy would certainly have worn gloves.

As Apple drove off, he gave his mind back to the present project. He mused that, in any case, the second of his possibilities was the best, even if, thanks to McKay, he hadn't seen how he could make contact with the bootleggers: through the man who went to feed the pigs. He, obviously, had to be part of the gang. If he could be located.

That proved satisfyingly simple, though not surprisingly so. Apple stopped at the first cottage along the road. He asked a young couple there if they knew where he could find the pig food man who drove by every day; he had dropped something of value.

Old Jock lived on a smallholding, the couple said, both talking at once and giving directions. They said he was a funny one, that old Jock. Never bothered with nobody, he didn't, they said. Stand-offish, you might say, he was, they said, old Jock.

That was only natural, Apple thought as he drove on. If you were involved with nefarious doings, you didn't encourage social overtures.

Following directions, Apple turned off on a road this side of town and went along a series of lanes. Eventually, his lights picked out a whitewashed cottage that would have looked its four hundred years if it hadn't been for the television aerial on the roof.

Apple brought his Austin to a halt beside the gate. Three yards beyond it was a door and one lighted window. Ready for immediate flight, clutch in and gear slotted, Apple shattered the country silence by pressing the horn.

He broke off to quail inside at his crudeness; then, with a vague gesture of apology at the darkness, he went back to horn-pressing.

The curtains in the window jerked. Seconds after that the door drew inward, revealing a bent man with shaggy white hair and beard. Even though the noise had stopped, he bellowed in asking what the pungency was going on here.

Apple rolled the window down and leaned his head out. He said, speaking quickly, "I'm the long streak of misery. You'll have heard of me by now. Right?"

Old Jock said, "No."

"Yes. So listen. I want a telephone number. One of the bosses' numbers. Maybe the one of the man in tweed with the funny cough. The man I saw today in the pigpen distillery. You understand, Jock?"

Following a pause, the old man said, "No, I don't." He started to close the door.

"Listen, dammit," Apple snapped. "I'm not asking you for names. Just give me one telephone number. And if I don't get it, I'm going straight from here to the police station." He revved the motor loudly. "The choice is yours, Jock."

The old man brought a hand up to his beard. After two strokes he gave a string of numerals, spitting each one out as though it were sour.

"Again, please."

Jock repeated the number, spittle flying.

"Thanks," Apple said as he released the clutch. His Austin shot away. Glancing in the rear-view mirror, he saw old Jock peering out from his doorway.

Minutes later, in a telephone-box in town, Apple was dialling the number. The call-signal rang. It ended with a curt "Yes?"

"This is Tim Gordon," Apple said. "Now get this straight. I am not interested in your underground activities. That must be obvious, otherwise the police would have been on your doorstep hours ago. Right?"

There was no answer from the other end. Which, Apple supposed, meant that the listener wasn't overly impressed.

"Are you still there?"

The reply was another curt "Yes."

Apple, having got a crafty, said, "You have nothing to fear from me. But, of course, nobody does anything for free in this world. So listen. I'd like you to send me a crate of your product. Just one will do. A dozen bottles. Okay? Fine. Thank you and good night."

That was better, Apple thought as he disconnected. The bootleggers would feel more secure, more convinced of his continuing silence, if they had, in a sense, paid him. At least theory said so. Practice often had other ideas.

Smiling gamely, Apple left the telephone-box and returned to his van.

SIX

Next day, in blazing sunshine, mist a memory, filming on the location went so well that Cookie said it was the calm before the storm. Everyone else said it meant that things would go smoothly from here on.

Apple tended to agree with the mass. He had the feeling that the mission was entering its final phase.

Which feeling was only one of several. They persisted as the day went on, conveniently for Apple. He was thus able to avoid giving the heavier ones his total attention.

Worry. That was on account of the bootleggers. Apple kept on the nervous alert, never stood far from other people, held Monico on a leash, and constantly half-expected to see Goon slink into view.

Hope. That was in respect of Helen Parker, who, with Miranda Wheldon not on call, was today's queen of the location. Apple was smitten and randy. He stayed hopeful that the supporting actress would pay him some attention; that they might exchange secret-sharing smiles; that she would intimate that their relationship was viable.

Guilt. That was because of the mission. Apple increasingly felt that he hadn't been pursuing it with enough fervour. To rectify this he kept a close watch on security man Wilson Croft and wrangler Chuck Holt.

Relief. That was connected with Velma Wilde's absence today from the location. Apple had no notion of how he ought to respond to the bit player when next they met. Her desirability had been dimmed by Helen Parker.

Pride. That was for Monico. Apple stood with shoulders squared as he watched his dog go faultlessly through shot after shot, be it chasing a horse or scratching at a door.

Desire. That, common to most men, was in relation to romance, though strictly of the non-physical variety. Apple wanted someone to know of his conquests.

This last emotion was the weakest of all, for, unlike the others, it wasn't recognised and accepted. Apple, in fact, would have been shocked if he had known of its existence, if he had known why, whenever he got into conversation with somebody, he began to broach the subject of sex.

The caterer's van arrived. Apple doubted if Clever Freddy would try his doping routine again, since he surely was aware that Tim Gordon was on to it. In any case, yesterday's mist having given Freddy many free hours of searching time, he had no need to sneak this midday session.

Even so, Apple made certain that he was the last to be served. Nor did he take a single mouthful until most of the other people were already finished—and showing no signs of tiredness. There were, naturally, those who settled themselves for a normal nap.

The lunch break was almost over when Helen Parker came wandering by. Apple's smittenship allowed him to excuse her attitude: lady of the manor visiting her peasants. After all, it went with the gorgeous costume, and her whimsical smile seemed to say, "Sorry, folks, but if you were in my place you'd be the same."

Halting near where Apple stood eating his dessert of strawberries with cream, the supporting actress said in a carrying tone, "Congratulations again, Mr. Gordon. Your dog is a great performer. It's a pleasure to work with real pros."

Some of those in the vicinity gave pretend cheers, Monico

wagged his tail and Apple said, "Thank you, Miss Parker. That goes both ways. We'd be delighted to perform with you anytime. Anytime at all. You only have to say the word."

The *double entendre,* Apple saw, had registered, for after giving a graceful bow, and before gliding on her way, Helen Parker held his gaze for a meaningful period.

Apple looked down from watching her departure when he felt a touch on his arm. It was Cookie. She nodded at his dish of dessert.

"You're slow at eating today, son," she said. "And you need to keep your strength up."

Apple wondered if, not too strangely, his adventure at the King's Messenger was already general knowledge, as well as his dalliance with Velma Wilde. But next Apple experienced disappointment (without knowing why) on hearing from Cookie:

"Strength to fight infatuation, I mean. You shouldn't waste your time trying to make out with actresses. You ought to know that."

"Oh, I do," Apple said. "I don't."

The retired stunt person shook her lemon-yellow ringlets. "They're the only pebbles on the beach, as they see it. Do you remember Loretta Prima?"

Apple didn't. He put a strawberry in his mouth and mumbled around it as he made his escaping departure. It wasn't simply the threat to his cover; he wanted to savour his hope.

Which reminded him of his guilt. Therefore he became even more vigilant in regard to his suspects. So much so that Chuck Holt began to look furtive and, at one stage during the afternoon, Wilson Croft came over to ask Apple what the hell he kept staring at.

Later, shooting concluded for the day, Apple found himself boarding the bus directly behind Johnny Fleming. The imitation property-man said, laconically, speaking convict-like from the corner of his mouth, "If by this positioning you're telling me that I should start taking the lead, I'll think about it."

Stung, Apple said, "I'm working on various angles."

"Sure you are. Slaving away like anything."

"Listen, smart boy. There's a lot going on that you don't know about."

"I'm not complaining," Fleming said. "Do you hear me complaining? This caper's a piece of cake."

"What with Velma and Helen . . ." Apple began, but ended there because he didn't know how to finish, due to not knowing how he had intended to. He was unaware of having rolled his eyes suggestively.

Johnny Fleming moved away with, "Oh sure. Just swamped by women, you are."

Apple's grumpiness in respect of that he was able to place at the door of his slip in mentioning the actresses. He wouldn't dream of doing such a thing consciously, he told himself.

Minutes later, when the bus was leaving Glengael, Apple saw from his low-slumped position that the pigpen appeared to be as normal. He took that as a good sign, though he couldn't have explained why.

At the guest-house, Johnny Fleming in mind, Apple went inside at stride, hoping to look busy. He also patted his pockets as though they were loaded with clues.

Half-way across the lounge, Apple came to a stop on seeing his first conquest. Velma Wilde, wearing a minikilt, was walking toward him like legs on a bundle of plaid. Her smile had width and warmth.

Arriving in front of Apple, the bit player reached a hand up to his shoulder and did a curvaceous semi-lean. In looking down from her face to abnegate the attraction he was feeling, Apple found that he was staring into her cleavage.

He went back to the face, though only as a way station

before glancing around the room. Johnny Fleming, not watching, was on his way upstairs.

Apple returned to the face to say, "Velma. Listen. I have something to tell you."

Smiling on, the bit player roamed his face with her eyes. "Yes, Tim. What?"

"It's about horses."

"I'll never forget that as long as I live."

"Yes, but what I want to say is, horses, you know, will go to extraordinary lengths to avoid stepping on a human being." He cleared his throat. "So I've heard."

"You know some fascinating things, Tim," Velma said. "You can tell me more, later."

Apple asked, "Er, later?"

"In the bar after dinner. Like before. Remember?"

"Oh yes. Yes I do."

"Then goodbye for now," Velma said.

"Goodbye, goodbye," Apple told her cleavage, and similarly gave a nod to the back of each long leg as the bit player, swinging around stylishly, began to sway away. The nods meant that he would be there.

His mind hazy, thoughts of Helen Parker confusing the issue, which was that Velma hadn't been prompted by gratitude, Apple went on towards the stairs.

He came more alert when he heard his cover-name being called out. The voice originated at the reception desk, which, he saw, he was passing. He went across.

The proprietress told him briskly, "Something been left here for you, Mr. Gordon." She brought up and put onto the desk a package and an envelope. "Both came by private messengers."

Apple thanked her and left. It was the heavy package that got his attention on the way upstairs. It was the size of a coffee-table book, and his name on the wrapper had been written in block capitals.

In his room Apple hesitated. Could the package, he wondered, be a bomb? Should he put it in water before opening, or should he not try opening it at all, simply take it away in the wilds and bury it?

Apple brought the mystery package (there was no information on the sender) close to his ear and listened. Hearing nothing, he abruptly decided he was being ridiculous. All the same, he put Monico in the bathroom and closed its door before tackling the brown paper.

Nothing happened. Inside the wrapper was a flat cardboard box. Apple raised the lid with cowardly fingers. Revealed were the tops of bottles—small ones. A closer look proved them to be miniatures of a famous brand of Scotch whisky. There were twelve bottles.

Apple spent several uneasy minutes trying to decide whether by this the bootleggers meant yes, no or maybe, or if the present merely represented the Scottish dislike of lavishness. He still hadn't arrived at a conclusion when he remembered the letter.

Lifting it to see the writing at closer range, he got a whiff of an exotic perfume.

"The very first moment that my eyes met yours, something profound happened inside me."

"Is that a fact?"

"I swear it, darling. It was like music. A hundred violins seemed to be playing a beautiful rhapsody."

"That's nice."

"And in that precious moment I knew beyond a shadow of a doubt that we were destined to become something very special to each other."

"But you didn't say anything."

"I was staggered. My heart was beating wildly, like a bird in a trap. I couldn't utter a word."

Apple nodded, which wasn't easy when he felt like shaking his head. He had been here fifteen minutes now, sharing a couch, sipping a drink, and he still had doubts.

At the guest-house Apple had at first thought that the perfumed note could be a forgery, by the bootleggers, an attempt to lure him into an ambush—taking into account that he might be getting neurotic about ambushes.

Tweedy and Co. were not that smart or sophisticated, Apple had finally reckoned, even though the wording was simple enough ("Please come to supper at eight") and the sender identified only by initials.

When Apple had set off, however, after showering and changing, he was uneasy. He hadn't felt safe until actually inside the mansion, being led upstairs and having the maid point out to him what a good job they'd made of repairing that hole in the ceiling.

But knowing that the letter was genuine didn't make it or this any the more believable. Nevertheless, Apple's ego was working on it.

He said, "Yes, come to think of it, you did say something when we met. You made a charming remark about my height."

Miranda Wheldon touched his arm with, "No, darling, we'd already met, as it were, before that, from a distance."

Since at the moment Apple could hardly recall his name, he found it unsurprising that he couldn't remember that meeting of eyes. He said, "Yes, of course."

Smiling up at him, Miranda shuffled comfortably inside her silken, mink-edged lounging robe, which plunged at the neck and leapt at the hem.

Apple smiled back. He didn't care about bleach or capped teeth or cosmetic surgery or silicone. To him Miranda Wheldon was fabulous. He was enraptured to be here even though he couldn't understand why he should be.

The film goddess said, "But I wasn't sure of myself, my emotions, until you were here that night. Then I knew. Even though we haven't seen each other since, I—"

"Yes," Apple said helpfully. "I saw you the next morning. On the location. I tried to apologize for that ceiling thing. Generously, you wouldn't let me."

"Ah yes. We haven't seen each other *alone,* is what I meant. The way we are now. It's heavenly, isn't it?"

"Oh, quite."

"Two souls adrift in an ocean of the mediocre," Miranda said with a gesture like seed-scattering. "Souls who are on the threshold of discovery."

"Yes," Apple said. He experienced a twinge of annoyance at himself for repeatedly bringing to mind for some reason a scene from the latest Miranda Wheldon film, which he had sat through twice. There were times, he mused, when having a grasshopper mind was a nuisance.

The movie goddess put her glass of buttermilk on the coffee-table. "Unfortunately," she said, "this togetherness by our-selves will have to be brief. In a minute we're joining my house guests downstairs for supper."

Apple grated, "How interesting."

"Now don't sulk, darling."

"I'm not. I wouldn't dream of it."

"Good," Miranda said. Leaning closer, she patted his cheek. "And I must retire early on account of shooting in the morn-ing. But tomorrow night. Ah."

Perking: "Ah?"

"Tomorrow night we have a date."

Apple nodded. In respect of dates he was telling himself in defence that he hadn't actually told Velma that he would meet her in the bar after dinner. He wasn't letting anyone down.

"Tomorrow's supper," Miranda purred, "will be for just the

two of us. You and I completely alone up here. Do you think you'll like that?"

"Absolutely."

"But I simply had to see you this evening. I couldn't wait through another decade until we met again. And now that we've broken the ice, crossed the glacier as it were, our date will be all the better."

"I agree one hundred per cent."

"I do hope you don't think I'm too forward."

"No, no," Apple said, snapping on and off a look of horror. "Not at all."

Miranda leaned closer still. The neckline of her mink-edged robe gaped at the movement, fully exposing a breast. Obviously noting the nervous up-and-downing of Apple's eyes, she drew her reveres together, though taking her time about it, the while murmuring lazily:

"How good it is that we're not young and impetuous."

"It certainly is," Apple said faintly.

"We're able to do our discovering of each other at our leisure, aren't we, darling?"

In a whisper: "Yes."

"This will do for the time being," Miranda said. She reached her face up to his and kissed him lightly on the lips. "There. Sealed with a loving kiss."

Apple cleared his throat. "Thank you."

"We have a date tomorrow night?"

"We certainly have."

The film goddess pushed away and got up, reversing gracefully. She said, "Now I must change. Please make yourself at home. I'll only be a jiffy." Crossing her luxurious drawing-room, she went hummingly through an open doorway. The door being left open, her hum continued.

Apple got up. He stretched his arms. He felt wonderful, he

told himself. He next told himself that if he felt wonderful he ought to be smiling. He smiled.

With acceptance of the now and the future progressing cautiously, Apple strolled to one of the windows. Outside, the low sun slanted rays across the well-groomed parkland. A man, walking alone, cast a long shadow. Birds chirped as on the day of migration.

Leaning his brow on the glass, Apple let his smile fade. Ego wasn't doing too well in the face of reason. A vague suspicion was growing that . . .

Apple became aware that the lone walker outdoors was familiar. A clear-minded look identified the man as Service colleague Stan. In his security-guard uniform, he was plodding, eyes-down glum, across the grass.

Apple acted on the spur of the moment. With part of him observing in disapproval, he swiftly slipped out of and let fall his blazer, knot-loosened and discarded his tie, unbuttoned and took off and flung aside his shirt.

Opening the window, whose sill was just above his waist, Apple leaned out. He coughed loudly, meanwhile keeping a watch on the operative out of the edge of his vision.

Not lifting his gaze from the sward, the dark-haired agent plodded on. Apple gave another cough.

The humming from the other room stopped. Miranda Wheldon called out, "Are you all right, darling?"

"Yes, thank you," Apple threw behind him. "There's a frog in my throat." He coughed yet again—a raucous, carrying racker that strained his eyes.

But they were well enough to see success: Stan had heard. Coming to a halt, he looked across at the mansion. His trunk eased forward as, patently, he was taken by recognition. He stared. He went on doing so, his head craning like a vulture's, as Apple performed the yawn and stretch of a man who was not only contented, but satiated.

Miranda said from the other room, "There now, I think that's about it."

At the speed of a quick-change artiste, Apple withdrew and closed the window and began to dress. He glared at the bedroom doorway warningly. It did no good. He had only his shirt on, and still unbuttoned, when the film goddess appeared with, "I told you I'd only be a jiffy. I never kept a real man waiting in my . . ."

Apple grinned fiercely as Miranda swooped to a stop. From the gabble of his voice he was able to distinguish that he was explaining about having been taken by a sudden stinging rash, caused, he supposed, by his fit of coughing.

"Why, yes," Miranda Wheldon, coming on, said. "I see it now. You've gone a terrible red."

When his telephone rang next morning, it was to give him the news that although it was a glorious sunny day, shooting had been cancelled. The star-director was sick.

Apple got the rest of it at breakfast in the dining-room, where he shared a table with the only crew members not having a lie-in. Daniel Range, they said, had celebrated so thoroughly his good day's shooting that he now had a raging hangover.

"Talking of gods," a grip said to Apple. "What was that you were saying yesterday about virility?"

Apple, his ego beating its chest, passed the question off with a casual "Don't remember." He might next have made his eyelids heavy if it hadn't been for the reminder of yesterday evening at the mansion.

But Apple insisted on recalling the informal, pleasant meal with Miranda and her house guests before getting to the real nub: his blushing attack earlier. And he then pretended that his embarrassment had been due to discovery in a half-undressed state, before admitting that its true cause was for what he had been doing to a lady's reputation. That the act he had put on for agent Stan had been a lie rendered his betrayal all the worse.

Apple ate quickly to busy his mind. It helped, so that he was able to slow again as breakfast went on. His ego being on the defensive, however, he started to feel twinges of the suspicion which had visited last night while waiting for Miranda to change.

That it was nameless aided Apple in soothing the suspicion away. Yet it returned intermittently throughout the morning as he walked Monico, spied on Wilson Croft, covertly watched McKay plant four rows of seedlings, and kept an eye out for his non-espionage enemies.

But in respect of the bootleggers Apple felt a shade safer. He reckoned that the longer they were left untroubled by the police, the more persuaded they would become of his silence.

At one stage late morning, in swiftly rounding a corner to avoid a meeting with Velma Wilde, Apple came across Johnny Fleming, who looked beyond him with a smile.

He asked, "How's the love life?"

"I've given it up completely," Apple said, stern. "I was only joking anyway. Would I waste precious time playing around with women?" He walked on, tossing back, "I'm not even going to concentrate on one of the three."

"You sound serious."

"I am."

Half an hour later, while watching from the dining-room window McKay plant yet another row of seedlings, Apple heard a fuss in the lobby. He went out.

From three cheerful informers, including Cookie, he received the tidings that the whole production team, cast and crew, had been invited to lunch, at once, in the town hotel. The hostess was Helen Parker.

Apple: "What's the occasion?"

"Nothing whatever, Tim," Cookie said, as though he ought to know better than ask. "She's trying to upstage Miranda."

Wondering blasély if this was perhaps the actress's way of getting to see him, Apple said murmuringly, "Maybe there's some other reason."

"What, for instance?"

"Well . . . um . . ."

Cookie asked, "Coming in the bus, Tim?"

"No, thanks," Apple said, leaving. "There's something I want to do first."

What he wanted to do was the reverse of a first. He had decided that he should be the last to leave—in order to make sure that all the others went in the right direction.

This Apple accomplished by peering from his bedroom window. The bus and other vehicles left, all heading for town. Finally, only McKay remained, toiling on over his work.

Apple gave the gardener another ten minutes. Then, McKay showing no signs of quitting, never mind leaving, he locked Monico in the room and left.

The sun was brilliant, the road quiet. Apple drove at speed. He was comfortably alert, pleasingly expectant. While he reckoned that the bootlegger danger was growing more remote with every passing minute, he again felt that matters were drawing to a close. He hummed "The Last Round-up."

Soon Apple came onto a winding section of road, with crumbly hedges on either side. Although he admired the prettiness of the scenery hereabouts, he didn't slow.

It was the drawing to a close of the caper which spurred him on, he assured himself, not the chance to see the gorgeous and available . . .

It happened suddenly.

The dread and nightmare of every motorist: a child running out into the road.

Apple had started braking and battling the wheel around, his heart in a thunder, before he saw the truth.

What he had glimpsed and taken for real was only a dummy. A crude one, furthermore, made hastily from sticks and draped in bright material. It was already falling from its push through the hedge.

But Apple couldn't give his attention that way—in hopes of pin-pointing the culprit. He was careening at speed toward the hedge on the other side.

He hit it, yet with relief. Compared to what might have been, smashing through a hedge was a joke. Besides, the event had in it something like the comfort of habit.

Next, hedge left behind and flying debris clearing from the windshield, Apple saw that he was heading directly for a thick-trunked tree. Which made him aware that he had taken his foot off the brake.

This, he realised, like the wheel battle, was instinctive. He wasn't about to hang around in the vicinity when the owner of the dummy child could be waiting to try again, perhaps with a double-barrelled shotgun.

With another wrench at the steering-wheel, Apple managed to miss the tree, though he was close enough to it to knock off his side-mirror.

There were more hefty trunks to be swerved around, plus the odd rock to be avoided and heather to be clattered through, before he was out in the open field.

Apple changed gear, put his foot down hard on the power. The battered and twig-festooned van shot away. It bounced like a puppy, thudding Apple's head on the roof. He didn't care.

The field, hemmed by walls on its inner boundaries, was a stretched-out acre running alongside the road. Apple drove by the farther wall, which, he mused, he could climb if it seemed as though he was trapped.

After having taken several fast looks back, Apple now had a longer stare. He could see the gap where he had come through the hedge. Beyond it, there were no signs of life.

Nevertheless, Apple kept on going as fast as the terrain would allow. He put one hand on the roof to hold himself down in his seat.

At the field's outside corner, hedge met wall with a five-barred gate. It was closed.

Apple stopped nearby. Although he was anxious to get away from the area, he had no wish to present himself as a target. On the other hand, the gate wouldn't open itself. He got out of his van slowly, leaving the motor running.

With his eyes darting everywhere, Apple went in cautious strides to the gate. The slightest noise would have sent him into a belly-flop to the ground. He could still see nothing suspicious. Latch lifted, he heaved the gate back. It swung wide open.

Apple walked backwards to the Austin. He got inside the same way. Even before he got the door closed, he had started driving forward. He shot gratefully through the space and sped off along the road.

The room at the King's Messenger that was available for private functions lay along a passage and through a curtained doorway. Seated at twenty-odd tables, noisily, were some seventy guests, with their hostess prominent at the far end. Helen Parker sat with her particular cronies.

As Apple headed in that direction to pay his social dues, skirting the close-set tables, he was acutely aware of being the focus of every eye, just as he hadn't missed the reduction in talk when he had entered. The looks were expectant. Apple felt the same way.

Helen Parker offered a hand for kissing. "How kind of you to come, Mr. Gordon. Finally."

"I had a little trouble on the road," Apple mumbled against a knuckle. "Thank you for the invitation."

With their heads close, the supporting actress whispered, "This whole thing is really only for you, Tim."

"I'm overwhelmed."

In a louder voice: "I believe you'll find your place over there. Table six. Do enjoy yourself."

Straightening, Apple moved away. With the niceties having been taken care of, he was now able to acknowledge others who were present, beginning with Miranda Wheldon.

He exchanged smiles with the screen goddess, who was sitting with her entourage near a window, the drapes of which were moving in a draught. Apple made his smile formal—then warmer as Miranda blew him a lavish kiss. That earned a few murmurs and hisses.

Tonight, Apple mused. It was almost a question.

The next person he noticed was his colleague. Rex, the fair-haired agent, along with half a dozen real waiters, was serving soup. No recognition was offered either way. Rex appeared to be depressed.

Humming quietly, Apple exchanged waves with Cookie. The retired stunt person, silver-wigged, sat at a far table beside Johnny Fleming, whom Apple ignored.

Arthur Reed, immaculately dressed, got up to a stoop as Apple passed his place. They shook hands. The production man said, as though expressing a hope, "I do so enjoy these nice *quiet* lunches, don't you?"

"The quieter the better," Apple said, squeezing by. He needed action like he needed lifts in his shoes. He was still not fully back to his normal self from that sick experience on the road.

The next pertinent faces Apple picked out belonged to the bit player and the security man. They were sitting across from each other at the same table. Wilson Croft nodded a show of disinterest. Velma Wilde sent over a long, searching, amorous look. Apple smiled floppily and went on. His ego was flagging like becalmed sails.

When Apple came to his place, which was pointed out to him by several people, he found that it was beside Chuck Holt. The wrangler wore his stetson politely on the back of his head. He said, as Apple sat down, "This here wine's pretty strong. If'n I was you, I'd stick to the orange juice."

Apple smiled. "Thanks for the advice, but I've given up wine, women and song."

"That's good news," Chuck Holt said. He went back into the talk of the others at the table, which, Apple gathered, was about the two female stars. Had Helen upstaged Miranda by putting her in a poor place, or had Miranda upstaged Helen by not stalking out because of it?

The soup came.

While putting a bowl in front of Apple, the waiter asked, "It's Mr. Gordon, isn't it, sir?"

"Why, yes, that's right."

"There's someone to see you, sir. Just outside." He moved on after nodding in the direction of the curtained entrance across the room.

It wasn't who the someone might be that Apple thought about as he began to get up, but that up, in fact, he was getting —after having been seated for less than a minute. It would seem odd.

Arriving at a tall crouch, Apple stepped away from the table. He was aware that talk had eased and that once again he was the centre of attraction.

He kept moving. Those people whose eyes he did meet while holding his gaze mostly downward—they sent encouraging glances towards the ceiling.

Reaching the side of the room, Apple went to the doorway. He slipped through its curtains fast, with relief, but then came to an abrupt, teetering halt on making an identification of the someone.

It was Goon.

Still in his bully sweater, the big man showed empty hands disarmingly. His face showed nothing. He said, "Hello."

Apple got his balance, settled. "Oh. Yes. Hello." He hoped he only imagined that he flinched.

"I was told to deliver a crate of whisky to you."

"I see."

"Real ones this time," Goon said with a grin that was both shy and proud. "Not miniatures."

"You've brought them here?"

"Aye. I've put 'em in your wee van."

"Thanks," Apple said, cool now. "But you could've left them at the guest-house, like last time."

Grin gone, Goon said, nodding a confidence, "But then I wouldn't have been able to deliver my message to you as well."

"What message?"

With another nod: "This."

The underhand punch caught Apple in the stomach. With a noisy gasp he jack-knifed over the pain, at the same time being sent backwards from the blow's force.

"Tit for tat," Goon said. He went off whistling.

In a doubled-up position, Apple staggered in reverse through the curtains. His burst of an entry into the room chopped talk off clean. Some guests gave cries of alarm. Others cheered.

Apple collided with a table. Among shouts and the clatter of dishes, he fell to a sit. He immediately put his head between his knees to ease the pain and get his wind back.

Talk had bubbled back into being, and there were people standing all around, when Apple, recuperating, felt himself taken into a cushiony embrace. He heard, "There there, darling. Are you all right?"

Apple tried to nod, but all he could manage was a twitch of his head. As though it were a violin, his head had been pulled over level and tucked into the shoulder of Miranda Wheldon, who was beside him in a tall kneel. She echoed others in asking what had happened.

Apple mumbled the first thing that occurred to him. "Well, I tripped over a cat."

Miranda repeated this for the benefit of the others, and then shushed at the following laughter. She murmured soothingly while giving squeezes.

Now Apple had his breath steady and there was more pain in his neck than in his stomach. He was surprised to find himself dwelling on the fact that the bootleggers, evidently, had not been responsible for that imitation-child ploy. Which was a curious way to think when he was in the screen goddess's lush embrace. Or was it?

Freeing himself gently, Apple got to his feet. He drew Miranda Wheldon up with him, assuring her that he was in the pink of health.

Before they separated, after the confusion of milling standers and table-righting waiters, of talk and thanks and apologies, Miranda said, "Until later, darling," and Apple said, "Yes." He moved away.

Through the immediate crowd he came across the supporting actress. She was standing there with folded arms and an expression of light pique.

"Are you all right, Mr. Gordon?" she asked solicitously, as any hostess would.

"Perfectly, thank you," Apple said. "It was a cat."

Helen Parker said, "So I heard." She stepped closer and lowered her voice. "By the way, don't be flattered or impressed by Miranda's gushy attentions. It's quite obvious that she's in the know."

"Er . . . in the know?"

"That she knows who you really are."

Apple smiled warily. "I beg your pardon?"

Helen Parker had nothing more to say. Turning, she moved off at a stalk. Apple, however, could see a light in the mental distance. Logic was having the final sway over ego.

Apple went back to his table and sat down. Ignoring the wrangler's laconic enquiry as to when Act Two was due to start, he began spooning up his soup. He kept his head down, the better to concentrate.

Apple had no notion of the soup's consistency or flavour, but his next step had come to him by the time he was scraping bottom.

Although he hated to do it, Apple got up.

The buzz of conversation faded as everyone looked his way. Faces were hopeful or expectant. Chuck Holt, squinting up, asked if he was kidding.

Apple moved on. Smiling one-sidedly as though to hint that all this was not as stupid as it appeared, if the truth were only known, he went with shoulders rounded to where Velma Wilde was sitting. He squatted there below general head level.

Guests close at hand watched; some of those at a distance rose to see. The conversation was holding on at its new low range, a buzz like that of an audience before the curtain rises.

"Well, at last," the bit player said quietly. She performed a pretend pout. "I was starting to think you were avoiding me."

"I've been busy," Apple said, playing it crafty. "I hoped you'd understand. I mean, now that you know about me."

The pout went. "Mmm?"

"Now that you know who I really am."

Velma blinked, flicked on and off a smile, said, "Oh." She looked worried.

Apple said, "That's fine. No problem." He patted her arm. "It doesn't make any difference."

"It doesn't? Oh good."

Smile quizzical: "But I would like to know how you found out. Did someone slip you a note?"

"The telephone," Velma said, her voice even quieter. "It was this reporter. I can't remember his name. He told me about you and said it was a secret so I shouldn't pass it on. And I haven't. Honest."

"I believe you," Apple said. "What did he say about me exactly, this Scotsman?"

"He was English. I think. And he told me about you being this billionaire. Eccentric, he said. That's not an insult, is it?"

"Not in the least, Velma. Go on."

"Well, he told me you were here incognito because you wanted the real nitty-gritty. You want to see how movies're made because you plan to produce one yourself."

Sighing like a winner: "Quite."

Velma Wilde presented a Gaze of Earnestness to protest, "I hope you don't think . . ."

"I only think that you're terrific," Apple said gallantly. " 'Bye for now. And thanks."

Velma said absently, "Oh, that's okay."

Apple moved off still in his squat. He might have kept on that way except that people nearby were already beginning to exclaim about it. Rising, he went to his place.

The second course had been served. As he sat down to it, Apple chuckled in order to give Holt and the others something to think about. He attacked the chicken and salad with the hunger of good spirits stimulated by the appetizer of looming success. But the food could have been cardboard and he wouldn't have known.

So the three actresses—and possibly other attractive females —had been spun a tale by Clever Freddy to make the dog-handler someone to be cultivated like a demigod, Apple mused. Why? To keep that same Gordon occupied, of course, after the failure to remove him through violence and extortion via Monico-as-hostage. And in that connection lay the answer.

Apple ate busily—until he got an idea which he found awkward. But he followed it anyway because he was enjoying this. Unaware of being the object of covert attention, he ate on stolidly, the pace a match for the plod of his cogitation.

Apple was kept on the awkward trail by recalling in paraphrase the maxim of Sherlock Holmes: when all possibilities have been eliminated, what remains, no matter how absurd, must be the solution.

Apple put down his knife and fork. There was, he knew, one quick way of getting the answer—a brief telephone call. But he wanted to solve this himself; then he could get confirmation.

Turning to the wrangler, Apple asked him a question. Chuck Holt, chewing roundly like a steer, thought for a moment before replying, "Don't remember."

Apple got up.

The conversation, which had returned to its former mid-lunch pitch, dropped as smoothly as a siren running down. The sound of cutlery at work lessened to the occasional tinkle.

Head lowered, Apple went to where the production manager was sitting. He wondered if he had been wrong. Ending the trip in a rush, he squatted down.

He smiled pacifyingly. "Sorry to interrupt."

"That's quite all right," Arthur Reed said. His voice was as full of warning as a dog's growl.

With others at the table craning forward, Apple put his head closer to ask the question. Reed listened carefully and anxiously. The answer he gave made Apple laugh, for he had not been wrong. At the laugh the production man stiffened. Apple tapped his shoulder as he got up. "Thanks."

He set off to cross the room, circling tables and declining to meet eyes. As he went, he heard the odd murmur of encouragement. No one was eating.

Beside the bearded man in uniform-style clothes, Apple dropped to a squat. He spoke quietly, heard the answer, laughed again. This made it absolute, he thought, even without the clincher. But best to have it.

"Thank you," Apple told Wilson Croft, getting up. He moved away, skirted another table, went to the curtained entrance and through. Behind him, he left a pall of anticipation.

At a cowl-topped telephone in the lobby, Apple made his long-distance call. Only two minutes passed from dialling to disconnecting. But during that time he worked out how he was going to bring matters to a satisfactory conclusion.

In possession of the answer he had expected, Apple made his way back. He went through the curtains at a seemly pace, then paused over the threshold to look around. He was watched, intently, by everyone.

Of the three waiters present at the moment, none was the one Apple wanted. He walked briskly along the side of the room, heading for a doorway which stood behind a screen. Along with him he drew every eye, despite there being a tinge of disappointment in the atmosphere.

Around the screen Apple went into a large kitchen. He saw Rex at once. The fair-haired operative was putting slices of pie onto plates. Except for remembering the dialogue in the projection room of that East End house, Apple would have felt sorry for him.

He went across. It was easy to ignore the stares of surprise or offence from the kitchen staff, as well as that of distaste from Rex, who had looked around.

Apple stopped beside him. The operative tilted his head to an angle of enquiry. Apple spoke. Quietly but firmly, he talked at short length. Finished, he gave a nod, turned away with military precision, went out and back around the screen.

As he entered the banqueting room, there came a soft hiss of indrawn breath. The air was taut with anticipation.

Telling himself he didn't feel the least bit remiss for letting his audience down, Apple went to where Johnny Fleming was sitting. At the table he dropped to one knee. It made a change.

Fleming asked, "What's going on?"

"Pulling the loose ends together, old man."

"Of the caper?"

"Right," Apple said. "Want to be in at the end?"

Johnny Fleming snapped a nod. "Of course."

"Then let's go."

They rose and moved away, Apple in the lead. Taking a last look around at the guests, he noted their expressions of doubt, impatience, reproach. Even so, he wondered if he was going to miss the limelight.

He made an exit through the curtains. Johnny Fleming, following close behind, asked, "Where we going?"

"For a drive. Fifteen minutes. With a one-minute stop on the way."

"Stop for what?"

Apple said over his shoulder, "To close a gate."

With Johnny Fleming muttering about the brilliance of the approach and the awfulness of the stench, Apple led the way from pool to pool across the pigpen. All he said was, "Step exactly where I do." He had been similarly reticent during the short journey, answering questions with "Wait and see."

Apple reached the central structure. Stooping, he pushed past the dangling sack, moved on and came to the spiral staircase. He clanged briskly down after flicking on a light switch. Johnny Fleming followed.

"Here we are," Apple said.

Looking around acutely, Fleming said, "This, of course, has to be—"

"No it hasn't," Apple cut in. "And isn't."

"It's not the secret laboratory?"

"No. It's an illegal whisky still."

"Well, for God's sake."

"But what I need right now is a drink of good old water. The machiavellian stuff makes me thirsty."

Still gazing around, Johnny Fleming asked, "How did you find it?"

"That's another story," Apple said. From a crate of empty bottles he took one with a famous whisky label, went to a tap and began to fill it. "Suffice it to say that we're safe here at the moment."

"How d'you mean—safe?"

"The bootleggers never show up in broad daylight like this."

"That's something," Johnny Fleming said. "But why have *we* shown up here?"

With his bottle full, Apple went to lean on a bench. He swigged and said, "First, let me ask you, would this place pass as a laboratory to the non-specialist?"

"If he didn't poke about too much, yes. And after that marvellous approach, definitely."

"I agree. In fact, I don't doubt that it's because of the great camouflage that somehow or another the rumour got started about there being a secret laboratory in this area."

Fleming pounced on, "Rumour?"

"That's something you have to know," Apple said. "Something that I suspected from the beginning but didn't check on until just now. I called London from the hotel."

Impatiently: "Yes? And?"

"The laboratory doesn't exist."

"Are you kidding?"

Apple shook his head. "There is not, and never has been, a laboratory here, secret or otherwise. I didn't know it myself. But what happened is this. Angus Watkin picked up on the rumour and gave it strength. He had it leaked around."

"*He* did?"

"Right. Actually, it's a neat idea. And, of course, he kept me in the dark so that I'd act accordingly. That's pretty standard, if you're Angus Watkin."

Johnny Fleming was showing his impatience again. "What was the point of the rumour?"

"To draw a certain free lance spy here. There was nothing to lose, no secret to risk. It was a trap for Clever Freddy, and maybe one or two others of the same ilk."

"Well, I'll be damned."

"And it looks as though the trap's worked. At any rate, I think it does."

Fleming asked, "Meaning?"

"I believe that Clever Freddy's going to show up here any minute now."

"And what makes you think so?"

"I laid my own final trap," Apple said. "That was what my back-and-forthing at lunch was all about."

After absorbing that, Johnny Fleming asked, "But why here, of all places?"

"Because Clever Freddy is well named. He's wily and a half. So he might well get away from me. But if he does, I'll have the satisfaction of knowing that he'll sell the info on this non-lab to someone. They won't be very happy with our Freddy when they find out it's only a still."

"Got you," Johnny Fleming said. "So any minute now—"

"Ssshh," Apple hissed, at the same time holding up a hand. "What was that? Listen."

They cocked their heads like parrots. There was nothing to be heard from above in the way of the expected: splashes from someone moving across the stepping-stone puddles.

Apple lowered his hand. His automatic use of it reminded him of Monico. He was sorry he couldn't be here for the climax. But then Monico would have refused to get close to the smell. He was odd that way.

Johnny Fleming asked, his voice at a lower pitch, "So who is Clever Freddy?"

"You can't guess?" Apple said. "No, that's not fair. I withdraw the question. I didn't guess myself. It's the last person I would've expected."

"Give me a clue."

Apple jerked his head up. "I hear something."

The first sound of splashing had been faint. The one that came now was louder. Others followed, until they developed into an almost continuous dappling.

Next, a figure appeared at the top of the spiral staircase. Another one followed immediately. These two men, tall and sturdy, wearing dark suits and hats, began to come swiftly and noisily down the iron steps.

The first called out, "Nobody move!"

The second snapped, "Not even a bloody finger."

They arrived in a bustle at the foot of the stairs. As they came forward, the first man said, "I'm Jackson, Customs and Excise, and this is Detective-Sergeant Brown."

The other man said, when now they stopped nearby, "And you're both under arrest."

Apple: "Under what?"

"You heard. And no doubt you've heard it before. As well as the following: it is my duty as a police officer to warn you that anything you say—"

"Hold on," Apple said. He had stood upright from the bench. "You're making a mistake."

"You just stopped in to read the gas meter?"

"I'm serious. If you wouldn't mind listening."

"We'll listen all night," the other man said. "But first we take a ride to the station."

"Don't move!"

Apple looked around, to his right, to where the order had

come from, which was where Johnny Fleming stood. Apple saw the gun in the bland man's hand and said, "What?"

Fleming: "This thing is loaded, as the saying goes, and I'm a nifty shot."

"Come on," Apple said. "This isn't necessary." He went to go across.

"Stop right there," Johnny Fleming said, face expressionless. "When I gave the order not to move, I meant everybody." He was swaying his automatic to cover Apple as well as the other two men.

"Are you out of your mind?"

"Not in the least."

Apple, who had halted, allowed his body to droop. "I don't understand."

"That doesn't surprise me," the bland man said. "Now put your hands on top of your head. Yes, all of you." As Apple and the others obeyed, Fleming started to move sideways towards the stairs. He reached them and, without turning his back, began to go cautiously up.

"First man to come out of here might get shot," he said. "Try to remember that, gents, if you get an attack of the heroes." Twisting to keep the men below covered with his gun, he went on up. At the top he slipped out of sight.

From outside came two light splashes. The next splash was so loud and profound, and accompanied by so potent a gasp of disgust, that Apple winced.

Rex, the fair-haired agent, didn't lower his hands from his head until the wet sounds from outside had faded. He said, "So that's that."

Apple nodded. "The wrap-up." He leaned back on the bench casually. He decided against a yawn.

Pushing up the front of his hat, operative Stan asked, "And that, prop-man Johnny Fleming, was Clever Freddy?"

"Was and is," Apple said. "A formidable opponent. He richly deserves his nickname." Picking up his bottle of water, he took a healthy swig.

Rex, who looked as glum as Stan, tried for a boost with, "Well, we put on a good performance. He swallowed it."

"Yes, he did. I'm very pleased that you followed my instructions on how to play the scene." That had been in the hotel kitchen, after he had told Rex to contact Stan, and before explaining how to get safely across the pigpen. "Well done, lads."

The pair said in dull, dry unison, "Thanks."

"I'll drop a word of appreciation to Angus," Apple said. He took another swig of water. "By the way, if you want to sample this home-brewed hooch, you'll find some full bottles over there. It's a bit stronger than the genuine article, but it does have a certain charm."

The operatives shook their heads. They looked melancholy.

While they were lighting cigarettes, Apple said, "Our Freddy had me fooled for a while—beginning from car accident number one. That was when he pushed me off the road in my van. I rolled over a couple of dozen times. No damage to my person except for this collar-bone."

Lightly, he touched his left shoulder. "But it's a simple fracture. The pain's bearable. I'll have it seen to when I've got the time."

Apple wondered if that was too strong. It hadn't been planned, but had come to him on the spur of the moment. The drab-faced pair, however, seemed to be doing some swallowing themselves.

"Clever Freddy came running down to the van," Apple went on. "He probably would've finished me off right then, except that other people were coming. So he pulled a cheeky one. He said he was my back-up."

Stan took pleasure in commenting, "And got away with it."

"For the time being, yes," Apple exaggerated. "I was shaken and in agony. Also worried about my dog, who happened to be with me in the van."

Apple thought that possibly a truer factor in his easy acceptance of Johnny Fleming as a colleague was that he so closely fitted a personal idea of the professional agent. This thought was partly to avoid the reminder that he had failed to check if Fleming had the use of a motor bike.

"In any case," Apple went on, "this was no life-and-death mission. And I was enjoying my flirting with the ladies. So I let things slide a little, I'm afraid. I dare say I was unconsciously trying to make this fun caper last as long as possible."

The pseudo-waiter and the quasi-guard both sighed, the sound like a breeze through old trees.

Apple, relentless, said, "But I did play with doubts." A lie. "I did think it strange that an Upstairs-trained operative wouldn't know the meaning of a clapper-board sign." A lie. "I did wonder why I should have a back-up and you men not." A lie. "I did think it odd of Fleming to keep avoiding the others." A lie.

Apple pausing to drink, Stan asked with a masochistic twitch of one cheek, "Was it worth the risk to Clever Freddy, him telling you he was your back-up?"

Apple brought his bottle down. After a smack of lips he looked at the liquid's level judiciously. He said, still casual, "Absolutely. It had value with three heads. It established that I was his enemy, the man he had to get rid of. It got me off his back meanwhile—he, naturally, being one of my suspects. It gave him a possible intro to Upstairs planning and even the location of the laboratory."

Apple nodded. "And he had nothing to lose by trying. He'd already done that with several of the others."

"He had?" Stan asked.

"Just as I had my spy suspects, Clever Freddy had suspects

in the counterspy department. So he went to each one and said, 'I'm your back-up.' " That was the question Apple had asked Wilson Croft, Arthur Reed and Chuck Holt. "When he drew a blank, he turned the statement into a joke. Cookie didn't think it was funny, and mentioned it to me."

Rex, in feeble accusation: "Another clue."

Apple ignored him, saying, "I was one of the last he tried, and, the others being cancelled, I was a hot prospect. Till then I was a weak possibility because of my height. Which, of course, is why I've been used by Angus Watkin so often—on those capers that the rank and file don't hear about."

Stan dropped his cigarette to the floor. He squashed it out thoroughly underfoot while looking at Apple's head. "Anything else?"

"One or two points which you might find interesting. That gassing incident, for instance. It came about because you, Stan, made the mistake of hissing at me from a doorway."

Drearily: "Oh?"

Apple said, "Freddy-Fleming was nearby, heard it, and did it himself later knowing that I'd assume it was you again. That was how I got led to the room upstairs, and nearly killed." He shrugged. "This caper hasn't been without its piquant moments."

The man who had laboured as a waiter and the one who had plodded out patrols of the mansion's grounds—they had nothing to say, though Rex, before treading out his cigarette, made a shuddery sound before taking from it a final, deep drag.

"Making no headway in trying to get rid of me," Apple said, "our Freddy next tried extortion. He kidnapped my dog. How I got Monico back is rather complex. Suffice it to say that Fleming was the only person I told that there'd be a massive search of the area if the dog wasn't returned. That wouldn't've done his cause any good."

Stan tried with, "So you knew by then that Johnny Fleming was definitely Clever Freddy."

"Yes," Apple lied. "But I was working out the best way to deal with him. Also, I confess, I had become pretty well involved with the ladies."

More cheerful lies, these, for Apple wasn't about to admit that the female involvement didn't begin until Clever Freddy, extortion having failed, tried to get him side-tracked into romance by telephoning Velma Wilde, Helen Parker and Miranda Wheldon with the billionaire story.

And he wouldn't have known about that, Apple acknowledged as he took a long draft of water, if it hadn't been for Clever Freddy himself.

He had been told by the free lance spy where to find Monico, which had led to his discovery of the pigpen's double use, which had caused him to be captured, which had necessitated him hitting Goon to escape, which had made Goon retaliate later with a punch in the belly, which had brought the solicitous, loving attentions of Miranda, which had spurred Helen Parker into letting the cat part way out of the bag.

Apple brought the bottle down from his mouth. "To the ladies," he said. He drank again.

And it was because of that punch and that cat, Apple further acknowledged, that he had realised (a) the bootleggers were not responsible for the imitation-child incident, and (b) said incident had come right after he had told Johnny Fleming that he was cutting out women. From that point on he had started to collate Fleming's oddities.

"But today I decided to act," Apple said. "Our Freddy tried to put me out of the game again. That was going too far." He told laconically about the accident. He didn't mention gates. "So I called London and got the act together. I already knew about this place. It's a real still."

Rex asked despondently, "How'd you find it?"

"It became suspicious to me when I detected chemicals in the smell, to worsen it. When I had a spare minute, I poked around. I had a run-in with the bootlegging gang, but I came off best after a bit of rough-housing. No sweat."

"A gang?"

"Don't worry. They never come here in broad daylight."

Stan said, "Why didn't you get the real authorities here, have Clever Freddy arrested as a bootlegger. That would've put him out of circulation."

Apple said, patient, "Because, old man, being framed as a bootlegger would let him know that there *is* a secret laboratory. This way, let go and not chased by us, he'll stay convinced that the lab's a rumour. Which is what I told him I'd learned when I called London."

As though in an attempt to cancel out his last mistake, dark-haired Stan said semi-agreeably, "But you really called London to get Angus Watkin's permission to give us orders."

" 'Ask for your help' is a better phrase," Apple said, being kind, but lying smoothly all the same. All that the exchange between himself and Angus Watkin had consisted of was: "Do I have a back-up?" "No."

With that masochistic twitch again, Rex said, "And I suppose you know where the real laboratory is."

Apple raised an eyebrow. "There are some things that are best not discussed," he said evenly, lying by inference. "It isn't professional."

Rex shuffled his feet.

Apple took another drink of water from his bottle, made a mouth of appreciation at its supposed potency and said, "On the subject of professionals, I mustn't forget Miranda, queen of the screen. A true artist and a delightful person. We have a date later."

Apple held up a hand. "Don't get the wrong impression,

please. I wouldn't like that. There is absolutely nothing between Miranda and me. Nothing."

The faces of the two operatives showed disappointment in not being able to believe him.

"One doesn't like to give false impressions," Apple said, whereupon he knew that tonight at supper he would tell Miranda the truth: that the telephone call she had received from a reporter was a hoax: that Tim Gordon, dog-handler, was plain old Tim Gordon, dog-handler. Apple sighed at himself.

Then, cheering up, he drained the last inch of water, burped, lay his bottle down gently on the bench and moved away. He walked towards the spiral staircase as straight as daggers from eyes, saying lightly:

"Shall we go, gentlemen?"

About the Author

Marc Lovell is the author of eight previous Appleton Porter novels, including The Spy Who Got His Feet Wet, The Only Good Apple in a Barrel of Spies, How Green Was My Apple, and Apple Spy in the Sky, which was made into the film Trouble at the Royal Rose. He has lived on the island of Majorca for over twenty years.